The Theory of Hummingbirds

The Theory of Hummingbirds

Michelle Kadarusman

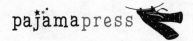

First published in Canada and the United States in 2017

Text copyright © 2017 Michelle Kadarusman
This edition copyright © 2017 Pajama Press Inc.
This is a first edition.

10 9 8 7 6 5 4 3 2 1

www.pajamapress.ca info@pajamapress.ca

 Canada Council Conseil des arts
for the Arts du Canada

 ONTARIO ARTS COUNCIL
CONSEIL DES ARTS DE L'ONTARIO
an Ontario government agency
un organisme du gouvernement de l'Ontario

Canadä

The publisher gratefully acknowledges the support of the Canada Council for the Arts and the Ontario Arts Council for its publishing program. We acknowledge the financial support of the Government of Canada through the Canada Book Fund (CBF) for our publishing activities.

Library and Archives Canada Cataloguing in Publication

Kadarusman, Michelle, 1969-, author
 The theory of hummingbirds / Michelle Kadarusman.

ISBN 978-1-77278-027-7 (hardcover).--ISBN 978-1-77278-035-2 (softcover)

 I. Title.

PS8621.A33T45 2017 jC813'.6 C2017-901874-4

Publisher Cataloging-in-Publication Data (U.S.)

Names: Kadarusman, Michelle, 1969-, author.
Title: The Theory of Hummingbirds : a novel / by Michelle Kadarusman.
Description: Toronto, Ontario, Canada: Pajama Press, 2017. |Summary: "Sixth-grader Alba is strengthening her
 left leg after a final surgery to correct her congenital clubfoot. Her friendship with intellectual classmate Levi
 is threatened when he scoffs at Alba's plans to run in an upcoming cross-country race, and she responds by
 scorning his theory that the school librarian has discovered a wormhole in her office" — Provided by publisher.
Identifiers: ISBN 978-1-77278-027-7 (hardcover) | 978-1-77278-035-2 (paperback)
Subjects: LCSH: Clubfoot – Juvenile fiction. | Friendship – Juvenile fiction. | Children with disabilities – Juvenile
 fiction.| BISAC: JUVENILE FICTION / Social themes / Friendship. | JUVENILE FICTION / Social Themes
 / Special Needs.
Classification: LCC PZ7.K333The |DDC [F] – dc23

Cover design—Rebecca Bender
Interior design—Rebecca Bender, and Martin Gould / martingould.com

Printed in Canada by Webcom
http://www.webcomlink.com

Pajama Press Inc.
181 Carlaw Ave. Suite 207, Toronto, Ontario, Canada M4M 2S1

Distributed in Canada by UTP Distribution
5201 Dufferin Street Toronto, Ontario Canada, M3H 5T8

Distributed in the U.S. by Ingram Publisher Services
1 Ingram Blvd. La Vergne, TN 37086, USA

For my mother, Judith Margaret,
with love.

Contents

Look deep into nature,
and then you will understand everything better.

—Albert Einstein

Chapter One

Wormholes

Hummingbirds can't walk. Their feet are too tiny. They perch, but never walk.

"Hummingbirds and angels don't need two good feet. They have wings," Mom says.

When I remind her that I don't have wings *or* two good feet, she just smiles like I haven't opened the surprise yet. I don't have two good feet because my left foot was born wrong. *Wrong* has a lot of different names. My doctor calls it *talipes equinovarus*, but I prefer the name Cleo. And it's not like I suddenly expected to sprout wings and FLY; but on the day of the practice cross-country race, something changed in my head.

Some days it's like everything is tilted; things shift and move around. My best friend Levi would probably have a scientific name for it, but all I knew was things felt different.

I watched Miranda Gray cross the finish line—her face turned up to the sky and beaming, her brown skin shimmering—and I wanted to run. I wanted to run, even though I knew, like the hummingbirds' tiny feet, Cleo isn't built for it.

Being timekeeper, I was standing at the finish line with the stopwatch in my hand, watching the runners stream toward me. It wasn't that I was tired of timekeeping and handing out the running bibs. I wanted to feel both of my feet spring and bounce off the asphalt in shiny new trainers. I wanted to be out of breath, laughing and bumping shoulders with the other runners. I wanted to be in it, not watching it.

"What's her time?" Coach Adams called over to me. He was patting Miranda on the back. "Well done, kiddo," he told her. Miranda was bent over, catching her breath.

My thumb was pressed down on the stopwatch. I read the time: 9:13. I called it out to Coach Adams and he marked it down on his clipboard. "Good work, Alba," he said.

Once the race idea was in my head, I had to tell Levi. The real race was going to be at the end of the school year—a couple of weeks after Cleo's final cast was due to come off.

Levi would know how I could make it happen. Levi is an above average planner. Levi is an above average thinker in general. I needed Levi's excellent planning skills and I also needed him to tell me I wasn't being coo-coo.

You could say Cleo is *directionally challenged*. I've worn casts and braces to untwist my left foot since before I could walk. I've had two surgeries, one in kindergarten and the second one four weeks ago. I used crutches for the first three weeks after the last surgery, but now I'm not meant to use them at all. I'm supposed to be building up Cleo's strength.

Not being sporty types is how Levi and I became pals in the first place. On account of my Cleo and his asthma, we've been thrown together a lot. In second grade we got to know each other, bookstacking in the library while the other kids had gym class. He started telling me random facts about hummingbirds. Like how they can see and hear better than humans but have zero sense of smell. And how they weigh the same as a penny but some can fly over 3,000 miles every year when they migrate. We still love hummingbirds, and by now in sixth grade we know pretty much everything there is to know about them.

At lunchtime I knew I would find Levi in the library. I peeked in through the double glass doors toward the IN/OUT bins. This is where Levi usually stations himself. Sure enough, he was there, sitting with his hand on the IN bin. He had on his usual worried expression, and he was staring at our librarian's—Ms. Sharma's—office. I slipped inside, feeling the hush of the room as the doors closed behind me.

"Hey, what's up?" I asked him, waving my hands in front of his face. He didn't move a single red hair on his head; he just motioned for me to *shhhh*.

"But I've got an idea," I said, stepping on his foot. "Listen to this."

Levi continued to ignore me. He pointed to Ms. Sharma's door. I followed his gaze. The office was dark and a Do Not Disturb sign hung from the door handle.

"So what?" I said. "She always puts that sign up when she goes to lunch."

Levi shook his head. "You don't understand," he said. "She hasn't gone to lunch. She's *gone* gone."

"What do you mean *gone* gone?" I said.

"She told me she was going for her lunch break and that I didn't need to finish the IN box," Levi said. "Then she went into her office, put the sign on the door, and turned off the light."

"So?" I said. "She went to *lunch*."

"But she didn't leave the room. And now the room is empty."

"No. You just didn't see her leave."

"No. I watched her go into her office and I didn't take my eyes away. I wanted to ask her if she knew when my book was going to come in, you know, the one I've been waiting for, the new illustrated version of *A Brief History of Time*. I wasn't sure if I should wait. But then I thought I would just go ahead and ask her because I really want to start reading it. So I went to the door and knocked. She didn't answer. So I peeked into the room. It's *empty*."

"But there has to be a rational explanation," I said. "You always say that."

Levi was nodding. "Yes," he said. "And the only rational explanation is..." He finally dragged his eyes away from Ms. Sharma's office and looked at me. "The only rational explanation is...there is a *wormhole* in Ms. Sharma's office."

Chapter Two

Big Ideas

"Good one," I said to Levi. "A wormhole."

I tapped my head to help me think. I knew that a wormhole had something to do with Levi's new and burning interest in *A Brief History of Time*, but I couldn't remember what it was exactly. I also remembered Ms. Sharma mentioning wormholes, time travel, and other science stuff when she talked to us about science-fiction books during our last library period.

"So what's a wormhole again?" I asked him.

"A wormhole is a cosmic tunnel," said Levi. "At each end of the tunnel is a different location, in *space-time*."

"Well of course it is," I said, rolling my eyes. "So where would she *be* exactly?"

Levi nodded and a sly smile crept across his face. "Who can say?" he said. "She could be traveling through time and space like Doctor Who."

I picked up a hardcover book and knocked him on the head with it.

"Get a grip," I said. "I want to tell you something." I was about to tell him about my race plans, but I could see that Levi was not going to let the wormhole idea go. Before I had a chance to say anything, he walked over to Ms. Sharma's office and peered through the glass door into the dark room. "If we wait until the bell," he said, "we'll see when she reappears."

"Exactly," I said. "We'll see her walk in from the staff room and go back to her office. Besides," I said, "I remember Ms. Sharma saying that a wormhole is just a theory. An idea. Science *fiction*. Not fact."

Levi turned around and glared at me. "Non-believer," he said. "Every great discovery starts as an idea or a theory. Albert Einstein had a theory about gravitational waves one hundred years ago. An *idea* that today's scientists have only now proved to be true!" Levi sighed. "Do you know what gravitational waves do? They cause ripples in the fabric of *space* and *time*. Haven't you been listening when I've explained the basic principles of Einstein's General Theory of Relativity?" he asked.

I started to drag Cleo behind me, doing my best Neanderthal impression. "Me, simple cave girl," I said, sounding more like Cookie Monster. "You," I said, going cross-eyed, "crazy scientist."

Levi was unmoved.

"Why would she talk about wormholes and time travel all of a sudden?" he said. "It's too much of a coincidence."

"Because she was talking about science *fiction*!" I said. "Because you kept asking her about it. Do you really think she told us because she suddenly discovered a *wormhole* in her office?"

By the way Levi was slowly nodding his head up and down, I could tell that was exactly what he thought. "And then she suggested I read *A Brief History of Time*," he said. "She was giving me a clue."

"It wasn't a clue!" I said. "You wouldn't stop bugging her with questions."

Levi's eyes got small, a clear sign his mind was made up.

"Oh, brother," I said, flopping down into a beanbag. "Fine. Let's just wait it out and get this over with."

Levi lifted one eyebrow. "You'll see," he said. "Just wait and see."

He returned to his spot next to the IN/OUT bins and stared ahead at the dark office.

"While we're waiting, I want to tell you something," I said, looking at Cleo stretched out in front of me.

"What is it?" Levi asked. For the first time his attention was moved from Ms. Sharma's office.

"Um," I said, looking down at the cast that enclosed my left foot. Suddenly the idea of being in the cross-country race felt ridiculous. A stupid, stupid idea.

"Nothing," I said.

"And *I'm* the crazy one?" said Levi.

"Just forget it," I said.

Levi shrugged. "Okay."

I looked at the clock. There were fifteen minutes left of lunch recess and I hadn't eaten anything. "I'm going to get my lunch," I said.

"Hurry," said Levi. "She could reappear any minute."

I pulled myself up and out of the beanbag and made my way to the library entrance just as Principal Ibrahim opened the glass doors.

"Alba," she said, coming into the library. "I was wondering

why the lights were on in here. We're an eco-school; we need to turn off the lights when we are not using them."

"Levi and I were doing the IN bin for Ms. Sharma."

Principal Ibrahim glanced at Ms. Sharma's darkened office.

"I see. Well, it looks like Ms. Sharma is at lunch, so it's time to clear the library. Time to go outside for lunch." Principal Ibrahim looked at Levi. "How are you feeling, Levi?" she asked. "Do you think some fresh air will suit you today?"

"I really want to get this IN bin done for Ms. Sharma," said Levi, not talking his eyes off Ms. Sharma's office.

"Well, it can wait. We can't have you two in here without supervision. School rules. Come on now, out we go."

Levi and I looked at each other. There was no way to stay. Principal Ibrahim held her arm up, ushering us toward the library exit. "Come on now," she said with a few claps to rally us. "Let's turn these lights off. We're an eco-school, don't forget."

I motioned for them to walk ahead. When I got to the door, I flicked the switch and the library went dark. I saw Levi's shoulders sag. Principal Ibrahim walked farther ahead toward the office before she turned around.

"Do you have your equipment, Levi?" Principal Ibrahim asked. She meant Levi's inhaler for his asthma. Levi patted the bulge where it hung in a homemade pouch under his t-shirt.

"Good," said Ms. Ibrahim. "It's a beautiful day out there. Perfect for some fresh air."

Levi nodded and reluctantly began to walk toward the exit. He stopped and waited for me when he reached the doors to the yard. Levi hates going outside.

"Come on," I said. "It's not long until the bell. Don't worry."

"I'm not worried," said Levi in a huffy voice. "I just wanted to wait for Ms. Sharma."

But he was worried. I could tell by the way he held his hand over the pouch and his eyes darted around the schoolyard.

"We'll sneak back once she goes back to her office," I said. But there was no chance to sneak back because Principal Ibrahim was right behind us, walking out to the schoolyard as well. She opened her arms to the sky.

"Make the most of this fresh air, kids," she said.

We nodded glumly and slunk to an empty bench nearby. This is where Levi sits when he is forced outdoors. From the bench he is able to keep the school entrance in sight. This time of year the air is filled with pollen that can set off his asthma.

My stomach grumbled. Between timekeeping and our library stakeout, I hadn't eaten my lunch. Then the first bell went off and Levi tugged my sleeve.

"Look!" he said.

Ms. Sharma was coming out of the school entrance. She smiled and waved to us before making her way to the class lineups.

"It doesn't mean anything," I said. "She probably just came from the staff room. She looks like she ate a nice big lunch," I added, rubbing my empty stomach. "Lucky her."

Levi nodded. "See how happy she looks," he said, his eyes following her. "Incredibly, amazingly happy." Levi gazed into space.

"Like she has been in another world. A completely different world."

Chapter Three

Lying to Strangers

$\mathcal{R}$unning is not impossible for me, it's just...well, I don't do it right. Not that I've had a lot of chance to practice. Most of my life Cleo has been strapped into a brace or a cast.

Back in first grade, I wore a leg brace. In first grade you play a lot of games. My favorite game was the playground treasure hunt. We were given little baskets, and the teachers stuck paper clues on the play equipment and all around the playground. The paper clues had words describing the treasure, words like RED HAT or BLUE TOY.

So the kids ran around collecting as many paper clues and they could. After a few minutes, the teachers blew whistles and we all lined up with our baskets and our paper clues.

If we could read what our paper clue said, we got a candy. I loved it. I thought I was in heaven.

I knew I was slower than the other kids, but I didn't care. I did what I thought was running and found three paper clues. It was a blast. I didn't understand that what I was doing wasn't running at all.

Mom videotaped the treasure hunt on her phone, and when I watched the video later, I saw how different I was from the other kids. I saw the awkward way Cleo flung out sideways as I tried to run around. It wasn't running at all.

Anyway, I haven't embarrassed myself by joining in with games since then.

But soon it was going to be different. Cleo was finally going to be fixed and I was going to run like a normal girl.

At least after my last surgery I have a cast instead of a brace. Having a cast on Cleo, compared to a brace, is so much better because I can pretend. I can pretend that I've just had an accident of some kind. Accidents can happen to anyone. Something sporty and daring, like a ski mishap, a fall from a horse, or maybe an injury mountain biking. It's not possible to pretend with a leg brace. Wearing a leg brace practically shouts DEFECTIVE. But a cast looks like a temporary thing worn by daredevilish risk-takers.

I admit that I have lied to people about my foot when it's in a cast—only with folks I'm not likely to see again, like bus drivers, shopkeepers, and random strangers.

But it can backfire.

One day I was waiting for the school bus and a woman stood next to me. She smiled and pointed at Cleo. "Ouch," she said. "How did you do that?"

"Oh, this?" I said. "It's nothing. Just a skydiving accident."

"Really? *Skydiving*? That's amazing!" she exclaimed. "You went *skydiving*? What happened?"

"It was a parachute failure," I said. "It happens more than you think."

The woman squinted at me. "Wait. So you *jumped* from an airplane and your parachute didn't open," she repeated.

"Yep. I broke my leg pretty bad, but it will be completely fixed in a few weeks." I tapped Cleo and smiled. "It was just an accident; it could happen to anyone. Soon I'll be back to normal, jumping out of planes."

The woman nodded her head slowly and smiled back. "Hm, I see," she said. "You are one lucky girl."

The bus arrived and she helped me climb on board. "Good luck with the skydiving," she said, waving good-bye.

A few weeks later, when our teacher was away at a conference, Principal Ibrahim came to our classroom and told us we would have a substitute teacher for the whole week.

In walked the woman from the bus stop. Her name was Ms. Honey and she was probably the nicest substitute teacher in the history of all substitute teachers. She let us spend entire mornings cutting pictures out of magazines to make a giant collage.

She never brought up our talk on the bus, but every time she looked at Cleo with her kind smile I wanted to hide under my desk.

Lying to strangers kind of lost its pizazz after Ms. Honey.

Chapter Four

Cowgirl and the Nutty Professor

Mom picked me up after school because we were going to Dr. Schofield's for a checkup. Dr. Schofield has been Cleo's doctor since I was a baby. He is super nice and he calls me his cowgirl. The cowgirl thing came about when I was tiny and I had a miniature leg brace that I used to bang around, and he would say, "Whoa there, cowgirl!"

Dr. Schofield has two sons who are a few years older than me. I've never met them, but I feel like I know them because of the photographs in his office. I have watched them get bigger in those photographs. The lengths of their hair and their smiles have become different. Geffrey, the younger one, now has braces on his teeth and in the latest photo he is trying to smile without showing any metal. Michael, the older son, now wears his hair over his eyes.

Dr. Schofield used to have a wife, too, but last year she stopped appearing in the office photographs. I overheard Mom telling her best friend Alisha one night when she was over for dinner that he had gotten a divorce. "It's really sad," Mom had said. "All those years together."

Alisha had raised her eyebrows and her wine glass, saying, "A-ha," nodding and smiling. Mom had rolled her eyes and swatted Alisha with her magazine. I was sent to bed soon after, so I didn't get to hear any more about it. Whenever I ask Mom nosey questions about Dr. Schofield, she says, "That's his personal business." She always adds something more about being grateful to him, which has to do with our lousy medical insurance.

"Whoa there, cowgirl!" Dr. Schofield said to me when we went into his office. "How's that foot of ours doing?"

"Good," I said. This is what I always say.

"Have you been doing your exercises? Hm?" He asked, watching me. "Take a walk around for me."

I did a few circuits around his office. Mom sat down in a chair in the corner of the office, watching me too. She was wearing lipstick.

"Are you still using your crutches?" he asked.

"No. Not much," I said. "Just if I'm super tired."

"That's great to hear, Alba. "You're managing to put full weight on it, just as I hoped."

"This walking cast has been great," Mom said to Dr. Schofield. "It's made a world of difference, Alba being able to get around on her own."

"Good, good," said Dr. Schofield, turning toward Mom and smiling. "I'm glad to hear it." They kept looking at each other. I stopped walking and coughed. Dr. Schofield turned to me, looking flushed.

"Okay, let's see how it's coming along," he said, patting the exam table. "Up we hop, please."

I sat on the bench and swung Cleo up on the table. Dr. Schofield took off the plastic boot, which looks more like an oversized sandal that protects the cast. He examined my toes poking out of the cast. The fiberglass cast wraps around my foot and up my calf to just under my knee. The most recent surgery was my final treatment to help Cleo point the right way.

"Any pain?" he asked. "Any tingling?"

"A little." I nodded. "Not as much as before."

"Wiggle your toes for me," he said.

In the old days, when I was little, Dr. Schofield used to play This Little Pig with my toes.

"Looking good, cowgirl," he said, giving me a wink. "I think we're on track to take this puppy off very soon."

"For keeps?" I asked.

"That's my plan," he said. "But you know, true works of art are never really finished."

"Great," I said to him. "Out of all the doctors in the world, I get the nutty professor."

Dr. Schofield threw back his head and laughed. I like making him laugh.

He put the boot back around the cast.

"Once the cast is off, I'll be able to do anything, right?" I asked him, keeping my gaze on Cleo.

"Well, I'd prefer it if you don't try to climb Mount Everest straight away," he said.

"But, I mean, like...running," I said. I saw Mom straighten up in her seat when I said it.

"Once the cast comes off, you'll have to work on your physio exercises," he said. "But in time, I hope so."

"How much time?" I asked.

"It depends, Alba. It will take a while to get used to walking without the cast. Your foot, your ankle, and your leg have gotten used to relying on the cast for strength and balance. You'll need physio to stretch and strengthen those muscles again. The muscles will be smaller and weaker from being in the cast."

"But—," I started to say and Mom hushed me.

"Alba, listen to the doctor please," she said.

"Let's see how we're doing when the cast comes off, okay?" Dr. Schofield said, helping me down from the exam table. "The good news is it won't be like last time when we did the bone operation. That time, you were off your leg completely while it healed. This time around, you've been active during cast time, so it will be easier." He paused. "You have worked a long time toward this final step, cowgirl."

I nodded and put on my backpack, ready to go.

"Alba, can you make an appointment with Agnes in a couple of weeks?" said Dr. Schofield. "I just have to talk to your mom for a minute."

Mom nodded at me. "I'll be right out," she said. They both stood watching me leave, and I closed the door behind me.

I had to wait until Agnes was finished on the phone, and then we looked at the calendar together. Agnes is not the kind of person you interrupt. If it wasn't for the fact that

I had known her so long, I would be terrified of her. Dr. Schofield sometimes answers her with a salute and "Yes, ma'am!"

"How is Friday after next?" Agnes asked me.

"That's good," I said, thinking that would give me that weekend—cast free!—to start my training for the cross-country race. No matter what Dr. Schofield said, I knew I could do it. I was going to be in that race.

"Let's check with your mom, but you got it," said Agnes. "Here." She passed me her appointment calendar. I wrote my name in the Friday square and Agnes typed it into the computer. Then Agnes glanced over at Dr. Schofield's closed office door.

"So what have you and your boyfriend been doing lately?" she asked, typing and smiling at her computer screen.

"He's not my *boyfriend*," I said, making a face at her. "I keep telling you that."

"Sure, girl," she said, winking. "You keep telling me that."

Mom came out of the room. Usually when Mom comes out of the doctor's office, she has a worried look on her face and she stares at Cleo. This time she stole a look at herself in the mirror behind Agnes's desk. She took a deep breath and was still looking at herself in the mirror when she said, "Are we ready?"

Chapter Five

Barefoot Librarians

The next day at school, when we were meant to be working on our eco-project, Levi and I mulled over how we could get ourselves into the library over the lunch break.

"Let's volunteer to collect all the classroom library baskets," suggested Levi.

"But that's a lot of work," I said. "By the time we finish, lunch will be over."

"We'll use the elevator," said Levi. "You can say your leg hurts."

I nodded, but at the same time I was thinking that if we used the stairs, I could get in some powerful race training.

"We'll use the wheelie cart too," he added. "That will give us plenty of time."

"The elevator is for staff only," I said primly.

"Hah!" said Levi. "Since when do you care about that? Besides, we can't use the wheelie cart on the stairs."

Levi had the same bright-eyed look that he gets when he receives a new copy of his *Junior Quantum Mechanics* magazine. I knew it was impossible to argue. Besides, it was a good plan.

"Okay, you go and ask Ms. Sharma at first recess," I said.

Levi shook his head. "No, you have to come with me," he said. "There is a far better chance of her going for it if we both ask her."

"Aye-aye, Captain," I said, and it came out more testy than I expected. The truth was I wanted to get the wormhole drama out of the way so I could have his attention back. I wanted to tell him that my cast was coming off and that I wanted to run in the cross-country race. But I didn't want to while he was giddy about cosmic tunnels.

I missed the old days when Levi's curiosity was contained to birdlife.

We visited Ms. Sharma at first recess, and she totally went for the idea.

"Brilliant, helpful children!" she exclaimed, beaming. "What did I do to deserve you?"

Neither of us answered her, but I don't think she expected us to. She is always asking questions without expecting an answer, like "Don't you love the smell of pencil shavings?" or "Is there a better place to be than two pages into a good book?" or "Whoever said the library was boring?"

"Use the wheelie cart," she suggested. Levi gave me a sideways look and I pinched him for being a smarty-pants.

Once we got started with our rounds, we zipped around the halls and up and down the elevator. I had never seen Levi so motivated. He dashed around like a lightning streak. I nibbled on my sandwich and watched him fetch and carry like no one's business. My job was to push the wheelie. On our first return to the library, with the cart fully-loaded, Levi pointed to Ms. Sharma's office.

"Look!" he said, already out of breath. "Her light is off!"

I nodded and stopped myself from saying—again—that she was likely in the staff room. Levi went to the office and peered through the glass door.

"Empty," he said. "Let's hurry!" He was practically throwing the library baskets off the cart. "We have to finish and get back here before she reappears." I didn't say a word—just followed behind and picked up the stray books that he dropped on the floor in his frenzy.

"We'll leave this level until last," he said, galloping ahead of the cart as we left the library. "Come on! Second floor!"

"Levi, calm down," I told him, trying to keep up. "You'll give yourself an asthma attack."

By the time we finished the second floor and had unloaded the cart again, half of the lunch hour had gone by. Levi had stopped talking to conserve his breath, but he still had the same nostril-flared look on his face.

"We're nearly done," I said, "just a few more classrooms on the ground floor."

When we finally reached the last classroom, Levi was looking desperate. "Quick!" he said, grabbing the basket. "Only a few minutes left!"

"Chillax," I tried to tell him, but he ignored me and threw the last basket on the cart. Then he took over steering the wheelie and scooted ahead of me back toward the library. I looked at the clock on the classroom wall.

Five more minutes to the end of lunch hour. I struggled to catch up.

"Five minutes," I called out. I rounded the corner and banged into the back of Levi because he had stopped, dead in his tracks with the wheelie, inside the library doors.

Ms. Sharma's office light was back on, but her door was still closed and the Do Not Disturb sign was still hanging on the door.

"Oh, she's back," I said.

"When I came in, her office was still dark," he whispered, panting. "The office door was still closed. It was still dark. The room was still empty. Then the light came on...while I was watching! And then there she was, *inside* the office!"

"But she could have come in from the staff room before you got here," I said.

"But her door would be *open* when she turned on the light," said Levi. "Besides, I can see inside her office from here." Levi waved madly at Ms. Sharma's glass door. "It was empty."

Ms. Sharma's door swung open, making us jump. "Hello, children!" she said. "Look at all the work you managed to do. I hope you also ate your lunch."

We nodded, watching Ms. Sharma take down the Do Not Disturb sign. Levi was spellbound in place. I gave him a shove to snap him out of his trance.

"We'll just unload this last cart," I said to her. "Come on, Levi."

We pushed the wheelie over to the library book shelves, out of Ms. Sharma's earshot.

"Did you see her feet?" Levi hissed at me over a stack of books.

I shook my head. "Why would I look at her shoes?" I asked him.

"That's the point!" he said, eyes shining. "*No* shoes!"

"No shoes?" I repeated.

"She has *bare feet*!" Levi wagged his head like he was trying to dislodge an answer. "Maybe she loses them in the space-time shift."

"Does that happen?" I asked.

"The evidence would suggest it," he said, tilting his chin toward Ms. Sharma's office.

I stared at the pile of baskets overflowing with library books. Then we heard Ms. Sharma call out from her office.

"Hey, Levi," she said. She came out of her office and walked toward us, carrying a book in her hands.

"Look at what just came in," she said, handing the volume to Levi. "The book you've been waiting for."

Levi reached out and took the book in both hands. "The new illustrated version of *A Brief History in Time*," said Levi in awe, studying the cover.

Ms. Sharma smiled. "And the best part," she said, opening the book and pointing to the chapter index, "is that Professor Hawking has added a new chapter." She tapped the page with her finger. "Look," she said. "A new chapter on time travel and wormholes."

Chapter Six

The Edge of Reason

Levi's imagination had been pushed to the brink. On our way home from school, he staggered around like a drunken sailor and waved his arms around wildly. He could barely speak in full sentences.

"Did you...did you hear what she said?" he panted. "It's proof! It's proof!"

I shook my head, wishing he would calm down. He looked more pale than usual. He was wheezing and his freckles seemed to leap off his face.

"I've got to get home and read the chapter on time travel and wormholes," he continued. "It could be a code. A code to another galaxy!"

I watched Levi wave his arms around, nodding his head in deep thought. I knew that this craziness about wormholes was not going to stop.

How was I ever going to get his attention? How was I going to get his help with the race? How was I ever going to be a normal girl if I was spying on librarians?

"I hope you don't expect us to keep doing the library baskets every lunch hour," I told him.

"Don't worry," he said. "I have a new plan."

"Well, maybe I don't want to be a part of your plan," I said.

"What do you mean?" He said. "Why not?"

"Can't you just be NORMAL for a change?" I blurted. "Why do you have to be so WEIRD?"

"What?"

"The wormhole is a STUPID idea. It's impossible and dumb and it's making you nuts. You're getting yourself in a hot mess about it. And besides," I said, "I've got important things of my own going on."

Levi glared at me. "*This* is important," he said. "This could be the most important discovery in the world."

"It's important to *you*," I said. "To me, it's just...it's just...*nerdy*."

I should have just told him there and then that I had plans of my own. Plans to run in the race. Plans that I wanted to put into action. But I still couldn't.

Instead, I turned my back on him and left him standing on the sidewalk, looking like I had slapped him.

At home I threw myself into my leg exercises like never before. I have always been lazy about doing them because Cleo gets tired quickly. And it's boring. But Dr. Schofield had told me that the more exercises I did while Cleo was still in the cast, the stronger I would be after the cast came off.

It had never mattered so much in the past, but now the end was in sight. Cleo's cast was coming off and I was going to be in the race.

I put full weight on Cleo, swinging my good leg back and forward. I tried to concentrate on making Cleo stronger and stronger. I focused on keeping my balance.

After a while I collapsed on the bed. I swung my leg up and took off the plastic boot. My foot and leg ached from the balance exercise.

I stared at the cast. What was it going to look like when it finally came off for the last time? I knew I would have scars from the surgeries. I also knew that my left leg would be skinnier than my right, because it hasn't had a chance to grow the same. But would people notice? Was I finally going be normal?

The idea of being NORMAL hovered ahead of me like a glittering, shiny new world—a place that I had never been allowed into. Somehow I knew that if I could just run in the race like everyone else, it would prove that I deserved to be there—in magical Normal Land.

"Nice work," said Mom, poking her head through my bedroom door. She came in and sat on the bed. Our pack of ancient dogs followed her.

Mom works at a nursing home for seniors called Golden Elm. This is why we have a collection of ancient pets. Golden Elm won't allow animals, so the new residents have to give them up. Mom says it's beyond stupid because it's the time when they need their pets the most. So Mom hunts the pets down and we adopt them if we can. Sometimes she sneaks them in for visits. We've ended up with a proper menagerie. At last count we have two cats and three dogs.

There's Smelly the beagle, Alfred the whippet, and Frieda, a Chihuahua who has a bottomless need for cuddles.

The cats keep to themselves pretty much, which is sensible considering they are outnumbered.

"Look," said Mom, handing me an envelope. "Sadie sent you something." Mom sat on my bed and settled Frieda the Chihuahua onto her lap.

"Thanks," I said, opening up the envelope. Sadie is Frieda's first owner. We exchange things like photos, drawings, and stuff. She knows I have a thing for hummingbirds. Inside Sadie's envelope was a magazine article about how to make a hummingbird feeder.

Mom patted my knee and got up again, carrying Frieda with her. "I'm going to make dinner," she said. "Don't forget to write Sadie a thank-you note."

"Okay," I said, petting Smelly the beagle, who had decided to stay behind and keep me company. Smelly yawned, releasing a waft of his stinky dog breath in my direction. I waved the air in front of his nose. "Gross," I told him. He ignored me as usual.

I took a thin-tip marker and started to draw a picture for Sadie. I drew a charm of hummingbirds—that's what a group of hummingbirds is called, a *charm*. The drawing was to go with a list of hummingbird facts that I had written for her. Last time I sent her a migration map. I was on my final hummingbird, a ruby throat, when the telephone rang. It was Levi's mom.

"Hello, Alba," she said. "Is your mom there?"

"Yes," I said. I could tell from her voice that something was wrong. "She's in the kitchen."

"It's Levi," she said gently. "He had an asthma attack this afternoon."

Chapter Seven

The Fledgling Birder Camp

Last year, Levi and I had gone to sleepover camp together. It was a camp for kids who liked bird watching. It was called the Fledgling Birder Camp. Levi had seen the advertisement for the camp in one of his nature magazines.

We couldn't believe such an amazing place could be real. We had to go. We sent away for the brochure and launched a begging campaign with our mothers.

"Pleeeease, Mom," I said, showing her the brochure for the hundredth time. "Please. We get to study *real* birds and sleep in *real* log cabins!"

We were relentless in our attack. Our moms were defeated within weeks. They signed us up to go in the summer.

The camp was held in a national park about two hours from where we live. When we arrived at the camp, the rangers gave us our birding kit: binoculars, a bird identification book, a pencil, and a blank field-notes booklet.

The field-notes booklet, we learned, was to write down our data: the birdlife we identified and any other wildlife observations.

"Is this heaven?" Levi asked me, flipping through the blank pages.

We had lessons on how to properly use our binoculars and how to use the "clock" method.

The clock method is a way of describing a location, because it's not helpful to just point and say, "It's over there." Instead, you pretend you are looking at the face of a clock: twelve o'clock is straight ahead or above. One o'clock is a little to the right. Eleven o'clock a little to the left. And so on.

"I think I see a bright purple penguin," Levi said, peering through his binoculars.

"You're nuts," I said.

"Nope. Definitely purple. Definitely a penguin," said Levi, pointing. "At three o'clock."

"Nuts," I said again, looking through my own binoculars, trying to find it.

He wasn't nuts. The camp rangers had stuck some dummy birds in the trees to get us started. By the end of our first day, we'd filled multiple pages of our field-notes booklet. We even managed to identify some real birds.

On the second day at camp, Levi had an asthma attack. A bad one.

Usually when Levi has trouble breathing, he puffs on his inhaler and it slowly gets better. This time Levi kept puffing, but it didn't get better. I ran and told the rangers that he needed help. I ran back and held onto his hand, because I didn't know what else to do. The camp rangers called an ambulance to take Levi to the local hospital.

When the ambulance arrived, the paramedics said I could ride along because Levi wouldn't let go of my hand.

The truth is I never would have let go either.

Chapter Eight

Climbing Mount Everest

I gripped the telephone tightly. "Is he all right?" I asked Levi's mom. "Can I talk to him?"

"Maybe later, okay?" she said. "He's resting now. Don't worry. But he won't be at school tomorrow. I thought you'd like to know. Can I speak to your mom now?"

I handed the telephone to Mom and stood beside her while she nodded and said things like "Of course," and "No problem," in a quiet, soft voice. When she hung up, she gave me a hug. "He's fine now; try not to worry," she said. "But Levi's mom is wondering if there is anything out of the ordinary going on at school right now. He seems very agitated at not being able to go in tomorrow."

"Uh-huh," I said.

His asthma attack was my fault. I knew it. I never should have said the wormhole was a stupid idea. I never should have said it was weird. I never should have called him a nerd. "Um, we have our eco-project due, I guess."

"Is that it? Can you hand it in for the both of you?" she asked.

"I suppose, but I really need to talk to him about some of the work first," I said. "Can I go and visit him before school?" Levi had actually finished the project weeks ago. We had done it on the energy efficiency of hummingbirds. (Did you know that hummingbirds have the highest metabolism of all animals?) I had drawn a pie chart and done all the coloring-in.

"Let me ask Levi's mom," said Mom, dialing Levi's number. "I'm sure it will be fine."

I set my alarm an hour early the next morning so I could stop by his house on the way to school. Levi's mom answered the door and led me into the kitchen where Levi was eating breakfast. "So nice of you to come over, Alba," she said. "You two go ahead and catch up," she said. "I'm going to take a shower." She smiled at Levi and left the room.

"Hey, how are you feeling?" I asked Levi, sitting down at the kitchen table. He looked worn out.

"I'm okay," he said. "Just tired, I guess." Levi offered me a bowl of porridge.

"Yuck," I said. "I don't know how you eat that stuff." Then I remembered Mom telling me it's rude to comment on people's food choices.

"Sorry," I said. "I had some toast already. So tell me what happened. Was it really bad?"

He shrugged. "I didn't have to go to the Emergency Room." Levi clutched his inhaler and glanced toward the kitchen door. "Listen, we need to talk about the wormhole."

"Levi, I'm sorry about yesterday, but don't you think you should just forget about the wormhole for now?" I said. "Your mom is worried about you. My mom asked what was going on at school, and I told her it was the eco-project. I don't think you should be getting yourself worked up."

Levi blinked. "Worked up? Just forget about it? Why don't you understand the significance of this discovery? A wormhole is not something you just forget about. It may only be open for a short amount of time! What if it closes or collapses? What if it collapses with Ms. Sharma in it? What if she gets lost? What if she gets hurt? What if she can't get back?"

"Levi, please calm down," I said. "You'll give yourself another attack."

"It even says in this book," he said, tapping the cover of his copy of *A Brief History of Time*, "that Einstein's General Theory of Relativity offers the possibility that bridges, or wormholes, could be created to different regions of space-time." Levi stared into the distance. "Maybe she has stumbled upon a wormhole left open by an advanced civilization!"

"Well, why don't you just ask her?" I said.

"Ask who?" he said.

"Ms. Sharma. Just ask her where she goes at lunch. Ask her if she has a cosmic tunnel in her office."

"It doesn't work like that," said Levi. "She's not going to give up the best discovery of the universe to a sixth grader. She expects me to figure it out for myself. That's why she told me to read this book." He paused. "She is a teacher after all."

We stared at each other for a few seconds. My mind wandered and I played imaginary dot-to-dot with the freckles on his left cheek.

"Focus!" he said. "We haven't got much time before my mom comes back." His eyes darted to the kitchen door.

"To use a wormhole, you would need to warp space-time. But how? We need to find out how she is doing it. How could she—"

"I can't," I said, interrupting him.

"Why not?" Levi said. "Time is critical! Haven't you been listening?"

I had to stop him from getting worked up again. I took a deep breath. I gave him a big, cheesy grin and threw my arms open like I was on a game show. "I'm going to run in the cross-country race!"

Levi leaned back in his seat, looking stunned. "What?" he said. "What are you talking about? How can *you* run in the race?"

The sting was sharp and sudden. My arms collapsed into my lap. I swallowed and felt a lump catch in my throat.

"My cast is coming off soon," I said. "My doctor said it would be no problem." My voice sounded croaky. "He said I'll be able to do anything I want. He said I will be completely normal. He said I could even climb Mount Everest if I wanted."

I turned away from him, pretending to look for something in my backpack. Tears started to burn at the corner of my eyes.

"Anyway," I said. "You don't even look sick. You look fine." I knew it was an awful thing to say to someone who had been up all night trying to breathe. "But if it's so important to you and your nerd hobby," I went on, unable to quit being horrible, "you can look for the stupid wormhole by yourself when you get back to school."

I stood up from the table, breathing heavily. "But if you ask me, it's a dumb idea, and you're only making it up because you're scared of going outside."

Everything was worse. I had come to try and make up for saying mean things and instead I was being even meaner. I couldn't stop.

Levi didn't say anything. He just sat at his kitchen table, staring at his porridge, gripping his inhaler. He looked as fragile as a bird. My heart was pounding hard.

"I have to focus on my race-training, but I'll hand in the eco-project," I said. "That's all I came here to tell you."

Just then Levi's mom came back into the room. "Did you guys work out your project?" she asked.

"I have to go," I said. "I'm going to be late for school."

I didn't wait for them to say good-bye. I brushed past Levi's mom and made my way to the front door, hating the awkward way I walked. Hating my stupid limp.

I let myself out and walked to the school bus stop at the end of Levi's street.

In my mind I kept seeing the shock on Levi's face when I told him I wanted to run. His look of disbelief. His head bowed at my mean words.

The look on his face that told me I didn't belong in the race.

Chapter Nine

Now You See Her!

The kids at school aren't mean to me. It's not like in the movies where the limping girl gets teased all the time. Not at all. I'm the girl that everyone is super polite to but who never gets invited for a sleepover.

There was one time when Allegra invited me for a playdate. It was back in first grade. It was terrible. Her grandmother spent the entire time with us, following me with her small, wet eyes. She watched me like I was an endangered animal. She asked a lot of questions—like about my dad, whom I have never met. At one point she put her heavy arms around me and pressed me to her chest, tut-tutting, saying, "You poor mite." At the time

I had a leg brace and I kicked her in the shins with it. When Mom came to get me I said that I couldn't help it. "Allegra's grandmother tried to suffocate me," I told Mom in my defence.

There had been no more invitations.

The lunch hour drew closer. Kids like me are good at avoiding the playground. We know how to keep busy. I decided to go and talk to Coach Adams about the race. I had planned on speaking to Mom about it first, but now I'd gone and blabbed about my "race-training" to Levi, so I had to move things along.

"Hey, there's my best timekeeper," Coach Adams said when he saw me standing at his office door. "Come on in, Alba."

Coach Adams's office was crammed full of sports equipment, and it smelled musty like the gym. "What can I do for you?" he asked, looking down at his paperwork. He continued to fill in a chart at his desk.

"Um, the race...," I started to say, still hovering at the doorway.

"Couldn't do it without you, kiddo," he said, still working on his chart. "I can count on you, right?"

"Well, I was wondering," I said. "Um, the thing is..."

Coach Adams looked up from his work, peering at me, waiting for me to spit it out.

"I was, well, I wanted to ask if I could run instead of timekeeping."

"I see," he said, putting his pen down. "Come on in, Alba. Take a seat."

I did as I was told. Butterflies fluttered around my insides. I sat down slowly.

"Why don't you start by telling me how you'd like to participate," he said.

"My cast is coming off soon," I said, keeping my gaze on the whistle that hung around his neck. "And I'd like to run."

"Have you talked to your mom about this?" he asked. "Are you cleared from your doctor to do that kind of activity? It's a two-kilometer race, Alba. We need to make sure you will be okay."

"I know," I said. "I asked my doctor and he is fine with it." The lie rolled like a stone down my throat and into my stomach.

"Well, that's great, kiddo," he said, but his eyes still looked worried. "I'll miss your excellent timekeeping skills, but that's great news."

"Thanks."

"I'll need to have a note from your doctor, okay?" he said, returning to his paperwork. "You can drop it by anytime."

A note! I hadn't thought about that. Of course I would need to get a note from Dr. Schofield.

"And, Alba," he added, looking up. "Walking the race is fine too, you know, right? You don't have to run."

"I know," I said, "but I want to run."

Coach Adams nodded. "I understand, kiddo," he said. "Just bring me the note, okay? And have your mom call me too."

I got up from the seat feeling dizzy. The talk with Mom loomed ahead. I still had to get Dr. Schofield to write the note. But now that I had told Coach Adams, it felt almost real.

Running in the cross-county race, just like all the normal kids, was becoming real.

I left the coach's office and almost bumped into Miranda Gray. She was standing in the hall outside the coach's door. Had she heard my conversation with the coach? Miranda stared at me like she wanted to say something, but Coach Adams called to her and she went in without saying a word.

Coach Adams's office is across the hall from the library, so as I turned away I looked through the double glass doors.

I couldn't help but notice that Ms. Sharma's office was dark, the room was empty, and the Do Not Disturb sign hung on the closed door.

I looked down the hall at the other offices. Some offices had the door open with the light on. Others had the light off with the door open. Some doors were closed. None of the offices had the Do Not Disturb sign on the handle. It suddenly hit me why.

Teachers put the Do Not Disturb sign on the door when they are *in* their office. They don't bother when they go to lunch. After all, if the room is empty there is no one to disturb.

I stood thinking about this, looking into the library, when it happened.

The light in Ms. Sharma's office suddenly came on!

I couldn't have missed her coming in from the lunchroom because I was standing at the library entrance.

I had to tell Levi! Surely it could not be true that there really was some kind of tunnel in Ms. Sharma office? A cosmic tunnel? And if it *was* a wormhole, like Levi said, could she be in some kind of danger? How was this happening? My mind raced with ideas.

Then I remembered what I had said to Levi that morning, calling him a nerd. Calling the wormhole stupid and dumb. I couldn't tell him, not now. Besides, he had already told me that he had seen this exact thing happen.

He had told me all of it.

I just hadn't believed him.

Chapter Ten

The High-Performance Running Shoe

"Race?" said Mom, her forehead creasing. "I don't understand, Alba. What are you talking about?" Mom kept her hands on the wheel and her eyes on the road.

"I need some trainers," I said. "Good ones, for running the cross-country race."

"Okay, back up and tell me what's going on," she said.

"At school they're having the annual cross-country race and it's going to be two whole weeks after my cast comes off," I said watching her drive. "I've been the timekeeper for *all* of the practice races. I've been timekeeper every year for all of the races since *forever*. But this year, I can race because I won't have a brace or a cast or crutches."

I turned to look at the traffic so I didn't have to watch the crease between Mom's eyebrows get deeper.

"Dr. Schofield said it would be fine, remember? He said it would be much easier this time. And Coach Adams said it was fine too. I just need a note and for you to call him."

"Alba," she said, arms straight against the steering wheel, "Dr. Schofield said we would have to see how your foot is doing once the cast comes off. You'll have to do your exercises to strengthen your muscles. We have to see how the operation worked this time before you try anything too strenuous." Mom stole a glance at me. "Alba, you could risk damaging your foot or your ankle. You could end up having to go through surgery all over again."

"He said I could climb Mount Everest," I said, looking out of the window again.

"He was joking, angel. You know that," Mom said softly.

"But I *can* be in the race. I *can* run. I know I can." I could hear my voice cracking. "I've been doing my exercises. And I'll do the physio every day once my cast comes off. My foot will be completely fine." I swallowed. "All I need are the trainers."

It was getting harder and harder to talk. Tears were escaping even though I was trying to hold them in.

"Alba, you will be able to do everything you want. In time. But you have to be patient."

I didn't answer her. The silent minutes filled up in the car between us. The radio sounded suddenly loud.

"You know what?" Mom said after a while. "I think getting new sneakers is a great idea. You are definitely going to need new shoes. Let's go to the mall now. We need dog food anyway."

I watched the traffic go by, getting my tears under control. My breath fogged up the glass. Mom kept driving until we arrived at the mall. Then she parked and switched the engine off.

"Alba," she said. "Please look at me."

I took a deep breath and turned to look at my mom. She gave me a half smile and stroked my cheek.

"You have been a trooper about your foot this whole time. I know you want all the procedures done with, and you deserve that. But we have to see how this last operation turns out before you can think about doing anything too soon that's too hard on your foot. Do you understand?"

"But I know it will be fine," I said. "I know it will. Please, can't you just call Coach Adams? Can't you just call him and tell him that I can do it? Can't you just ask Dr. Schofield to write a note? Please, Mom? I've already told...I've already told everyone. Please?"

Mom sighed and shook her head. "I will speak with Dr. Schofield and I will speak with the coach. But I can't promise it will happen the way you want it to happen, Alba. I'm sorry. I just can't promise you that. But I will see what is possible."

"It will be okay," I said, throwing my arms around her. "I know it will. Just tell them I can do it. Okay?"

"I'll speak with them, Alba, but please remember what I just told you. I don't want you getting disappointed once the cast comes off."

"I won't be," I said, getting out of the car. "Because it's going to be fine. It's going to be totally fine." Every time I said *fine* my stomach flipped.

I didn't wait for Mom to answer. Instead I made a bee-line for the mall entrance and the shoe store. I knew exactly the shoes I wanted to get. Shiny orange, just like the ones Miranda Gray wears.

In the store, both the sales person and Mom tried their best to steer me toward the cross-trainers and ordinary sneakers, but they were no match for my devotion to the shiny orange high-performance running shoe.

On the way home from the mall, Mom asked if I wanted to drop by Levi's.

"No, it's okay," I said. "He probably still needs to rest."

I had my new trainers out of the box and was admiring them, holding them up to the sunlight. I pictured myself springing like a gazelle across the finish line. I didn't want to break the bubble. I didn't want to see the look Levi would give me again, the look that said I had no business running in the race. The look that said I didn't belong in Normal Land.

"I'll call him later," I said to Mom. But as I heard my own words, I knew that I wouldn't.

Later at home I added some little-known facts about hummingbirds for Sadie:

- Hummingbirds are not always as nice as they look

- They are not very social

- They can actually be quite aggressive

- Hummingbirds have even been known to attack other birds

Chapter Eleven

Field Studies and Pig Braids

May is the month I look forward to the most because it's usually when I see my first hummingbird. Years ago, Mom and I planted begonias, fuchsias, and geraniums that bloom with red flowers. The color red attracts hummingbirds. I also hang two red hummingbird feeders from our cherry tree as insurance. I put sugar water in the feeders on the first day of spring. It's wishful thinking, but who cares? The earliest I've ever seen a hummingbird in our garden was April 17. That was back in fourth grade. It only happened the once. Since then they usually arrive in mid- to late May and stay until the end of the summer.

It's been a cool spring and the hummingbirds are late

this year. Mom offered to take me to the butterfly and bird sanctuary so I could start my field studies. Ever since Fledgling Birder Camp, Levi and I write down our hummingbird observations in the field-notes booklet they gave us. This year I started on April 17 (my first-ever official sighting) and then each date after that. Each day I mark down the sighted activity (none so far) and the field study location (my garden). I add the conditions, like the weather and the level of the sugar water in the feeders, if the flowers are in bloom, and any other significant activity from butterflies, bees, and other birds.

"It won't technically be field studies if I'm not, you know, *in the field*," I said to Mom.

She shrugged. "True. But the sanctuary is nice and warm. And it's as close as we'll get to a tropical vacation. I'll bring magazines to read and pretend I'm in the Costa Rican rainforest."

This is how I came to be sitting in the bird and butterfly sanctuary in front of the small-species enclosure with my field-notes booklet in my lap.

"Does it hurt?" asked a voice.

I noticed her shoes before anything else. They were the kind that light up with each step. They were flashing bright purple with each impatient toe tap.

I looked up to see a very small girl with glasses, pointing

at Cleo. One side of her hair was braided and the other side was in a pigtail. She carried a thermos and wore a woman's purse over her shoulder.

"Abigail Pontifax," she said, her tiny hand outstretched. I shook it.

"Alba," I replied.

Abigail took this as an invitation to sit beside me.

"Don't you love it here?" she said with a sigh. "It's so peaceful."

I nodded. "How old are you?" I asked her.

"I'm seven. Second grade. That's my mom over there." Abigail pointed to a woman who was talking intently with another woman. Abigail's mother was gripping onto her friend's forearm and gesturing widely with the other.

"She's a therapist," said Abigail.

"Oh."

"So, does it?" Abigail asked.

"Does it what?"

"Does it *hurt*. Your leg," she said pointing to Cleo again.

"Oh. No. Not really. Not much anymore. I'm used to it, I guess."

"Hm. So that's not it." Abigail went about opening her thermos. "Do you want to talk about it?" she asked.

"What you mean?" I asked. "Talk about what?"

"I've been watching you, and you look sad about something. Your eyes have tears in them when you watch the birds, and then you stare at your notebook and don't write anything."

"Oh. It's just that I usually do this with my friend Levi. But...well, I don't know if he's my friend anymore."

She nodded slowly. "That's what happened to me and Simon."

"Who's Simon?"

"He was my boyfriend in preschool."

"Oh." I shook my head. "It's not like that. Levi and I are just friends. We've been friends since—"

Abigail held up her hand like a tiny stop sign and shook her head. "Doesn't matter. He's pretty special, isn't he?"

I nodded. I was becoming hypnotized by her flashing purple shoes.

"Coffee?" asked Abigail, offering me her thermos.

"You drink coffee?"

"Of course. Don't worry; it's organic. Fair trade." She took a large sip. "Decaf."

"No, I'm okay. Thanks anyway."

"My mom says it's always better to express your feelings," Abigail said. "Even if you don't actually say the words out loud. You know, you just whisper your troubles into a napkin so no one can hear it."

"A napkin?"

"Well it doesn't have to be a napkin exactly. It could be a handkerchief, or even a scarf. But not a paper towel. Anything as long as you can put it in the washing machine afterward. It washes away the bad feelings."

I nodded, watching her sip her decaf.

"Otherwise, Mom says, the feelings get toxic," said Abigail. "Here, try it," she added, taking a scarf from her purse.

"No, it's okay."

"Suit yourself," she said, shrugging.

Abigail returned the scarf to her purse and took out a notebook. She put down her thermos and wrote something in the notebook. She ripped out the page and handed me the slip of paper.

"If you want to talk," she said.

"What is this?" I asked.

"My phone number, "she said. "Call whenever you want."

Before I could reply, Mom appeared in front of our bench.

"Ready?" she asked.

"Sure," I said and got up to leave.

Abigail fist-pumped the air. She crossed and recrossed her legs, tapping her toes so they flickered purple. "It's been a pleasure," she said.

"Me too," I said, totally meaning it.

We shook hands again.

"And thanks for not asking about my pig braids," she said, rolling her eyes. "It's what my mom calls a *fashion compromise*."

As I walked with Mom through the sanctuary to the parking lot, she looped her arm through mine.

"Was that *coffee* in that little girl's thermos?" she asked.

"Yes," I said, smiling to myself. "But don't worry. It was organic. Fair trade."

In the car on the drive home I looked at the slip of paper that Abigail had given me. There was a phone number, and in large loopy square letters she had written: *I LIKE YOU* ☺

Chapter Twelve

The Supply Closet

Levi came back to school but we didn't talk. He hung around with his chess-club friends and we avoided eye contact in the halls. Even though we weren't talking, I kept tabs on him. Where he was, what he was doing, and who he was with. I considered starting a field-notes book on Levi's activity but realized that would make me a total creeper. So I didn't.

I kept up Cleo's exercises and started walking longer distances to help with my race training. Some days I watched Miranda and the other athletic kids run around the track, trying to pick up running tips. I hoped that if I watched the runners long enough, my legs would know what to do when the time came.

I visited the library often to make sure Ms. Sharma was still on earth. I covered this by asking if she needed help with the library baskets. Maybe I did this a few too many times because she looked at me intently. "Thanks, Alba, but it's okay," she said. "Don't you think you should make the most of your lunch break?"

I wondered whether this meant that she had promised the job to Levi instead. Or maybe she had started to suspect we knew about her secret discovery?

I went to the school office to see if they wanted the recycle bins emptied, they said no need since I had done such a good job of it at first recess. So I tidied up the Lost and Found closet as best I could—which is honestly a total disaster zone. Next to the Lost and Found closet there is a large window that faces out to the schoolyard. I reunited items of outerwear—mittens, gloves, boots—and watched Miranda Gray and her friends play four square. After a few minutes, Miranda stopped in midserve. She stood up and looked directly at the window. She smiled and waved, motioning for me to join in. I took a quick sidestep to the right of the window frame, out of sight; sure that she had me confused with someone else.

Without really making a decision about what I was doing next, I went back to the library. Coach Adams was working at his desk with the door halfway open when I walked past. He didn't look up from his work as I slipped through the library doors. It was dark inside now and all of the lights were off, including Ms. Sharma's office. I made my way to her office and stood outside the door. Her Do Not Disturb sign hung on her door handle. It was so quiet in the library that I could hear myself breathe.

I put my hand on the handle and slowly opened the door. My heart was thumping against my chest. I took a step into the office. I looked around. The room was dark, but it was easy to tell that it was empty. I walked slowly around the room, holding my breath before looking under Ms. Sharma's desk. Nothing. Then I ran my hand over the walls, but all I felt were the paper posters covering the cool, hard concrete. I continued to walk around the room, running my hands along all the walls. Nothing. The only other thing in the office, apart from the desk, was the supply closet. I knew it was the supply closet because SUPPLY CLOSET was written in big letters on the door. I moved toward it and gripped the door handle. I gave it a tug but it wouldn't budge. Locked. There was definitely no secret door to the staff room, and as far as I could tell, there was no wormhole to another dimension either. The room was empty.

I stood in the dark office feeling spooked. Then I noticed a smell. A nice smell. Perfumey. Smokey and flowery. It was something I had smelled before, but I couldn't place what it was.

I slipped out of Ms. Sharma's office and closed the door quietly behind me. Then I stood in the dark library wondering what to do. I had to wait and see if she reappeared in the office like I had seen happen before. I stood next to the library entrance with my back against the wall. I glanced at the wall clock—just a few minutes left of lunch recess. Soon the halls would be filled with kids and I would have to go back to class. My heart was thumping in my chest. I could hear my own breath. It took me a few seconds before I realized that I could hear something else as well. It was a familiar sound.

But before I had time to think about it, the light came on in Ms. Sharma's office. I gasped. There she was! Inside the office! She opened the door and took the sign off the handle. But she didn't look up; she didn't see me. She turned and went back into her office, and I dashed out of the library.

The end of recess bell sounded and the corridor began to fill up with kids and teachers. My head was swimming. I turned it over and over in my mind. Ms. Sharma's office had *definitely* been empty, but she appeared inside a few minutes later. There were no other entrances to the room. The supply closet was the only possibility. But if there was some kind of wormhole or tunnel in the supply closet, how could it be locked?

Then I remembered the noise I had heard. I hadn't been the only one in the library. And I guessed that I wasn't the only one who had discovered the supply closet either. The noise I heard had been the pump of an inhaler. Something I had heard Levi do a million times.

Chapter Thirteen

Google and the Cookie Monster

The night before Cleo's cast was due to come off, to help calm my jitters, I Googled *A Brief History of Time*. I read phrases like *the theory of everything*, *big bang*, *black holes*, and *space-time* until my head was spinning, my brain ached, and my stomach felt strange.

Could it be that our own Ms. Sharma had discovered something that even the world's most brilliant scientists have not? And if she had found a wormhole, was she traveling through time, or to an alternate realm like *Alice in Wonderland*, or had she just found a nifty way to get home for lunch? What if the wormhole collapsed and she vanished, like Levi had said? Could a person fall in if they got too close?

I rubbed my eyes and lay my forehead down on the computer desk. The funny feelings in my stomach were butterflies about the next day, when Cleo's cast would be taken off for the last time.

I felt Mom put her hand on top of my head. "Time for bed, Alba," she said. "It's a big day tomorrow."

"Okay," I said, sitting up and stretching. I switched off the computer.

"Alba," she said. "Let's talk for a minute."

I turned around to face her. She was holding Frieda. She smiled at me and tilted her head. "Are you okay?" she asked.

"Yes," I said, more confident than I felt. "I'm okay. Don't worry."

"Tomorrow is a big deal," said Mom, stroking Frieda. "I want you to be prepared for disappointment if the operation hasn't worked out 100 percent. Remember what we talked about, okay?"

"I will," I said. "I promise."

Mom just looked at me and nodded. Her eyes looked worried.

I got up and kissed her on the cheek. "It's okay, Mom. Really." I gave Frieda a kiss too. "I'm going to bed."

I went to my room and saw that Alfred had beaten me

into bed. He looked up at me with a guilty face but I let him stay. I rearranged his spindly whippet legs before slipping under the covers. Smelly the beagle and the cats were having a truce and were asleep together on the spare bed. I turned off the light and closed my eyes. All of the information that I had read online swam behind my eyelids.

It was hard to fall asleep. It was hard not to think about what would be under Cleo's cast. When I finally fell asleep, I had a dream that I was falling through a hole. The hole became a tunnel and the sides of the tunnel were filled with books—shelves of books like in the school library— but every time I tried to grab hold of one, it disappeared.

I kicked my legs and flapped my arms and I heard some-one say, "Are you trying to fly? Is that what you're trying to do?" And then I was sitting in a tree, feeling foolish, wondering how I got up so high.

How am I going to get down? I wondered. I looked at Cleo. The cast was off but my foot was not a human foot at all. It was a huge, furry blue foot.

"It's okay. You're the Cookie Monster, remember?" The words came from Mom, who was now also sitting in the tree.

"But I don't want to be the Cookie Monster!" I cried, shaking my huge, furry blue foot. "Please! I just want to be normal!" I was crying and shouting. "Please! I just want to be normal!" I could feel my cheeks getting wet.

The next thing I knew, Mom was shaking me awake and Alfred was licking my face.

"Time to get up," she said. "Today's the day."

Chapter Fourteen

Cleo's Big Debut

Dr. Schofield held Cleo in his hand.

I kept my eyes focused on it to remind myself that it was actually attached to me. This small, pale foot, connected to the thin, white leg, was part of me.

"I'm going to manipulate your foot and ankle a little," he said. "You tell me to stop if it hurts, okay?"

I nodded and he began to turn my foot around in his hand and press it back and forth. He kept his eyes on my face. "How is that?" he asked. "We need to work on flexibility. Your ankle has been in the cast for a long time, so it will feel strange at first."

I nodded, my eyes still on Cleo. My foot was pointing

the right way. It was straight; it wasn't twisted. There was a new scar on my heel that ran up the back of my calf.

I looked over at Mom, whose eyes were shiny. I think she was holding her breath, because she was just nodding with her hands over her mouth.

Dr. Schofield smiled at me. "Okay, cowgirl. Let's see you put some weight on it." He helped me down from the exam table and held my hand while I gingerly stepped onto the carpet.

I stood on my right foot and tested the weight on my left. I took tiny steps and let go of his hand.

"It feels so weird," I said. "It's so stiff."

"That's natural," he said. "It's bound to feel stiff and awkward at first."

I took small steps, one after the other, until I did a kind of victory hobble around the office. I had to grab onto furniture for balance. I stopped to give Dr. Schofield a high-five. I hugged Mom and Agnes too, who had joined us. I sat down and lined both feet up next to each other on the carpet.

"It looks so...*small*," I said.

Dr. Schofield nodded. "That's because your left foot and leg haven't had a chance to develop in the same way as your right side. Your calf will get stronger, and so will your foot, but it will never look exactly the same."

"It looks perfect to me," said Mom, who had finally taken her hands from her mouth.

"Did you bring the trainers?" I asked her.

Mom handed me a bag with the new trainers. I put on a pair of socks and I slipped into the shoes. It was amazing to feel the spring of the trainers underneath both feet. I got up and put weight on each foot, one at a time.

"You'll have to be careful of your left heel because the scar at the back will rub and give you nasty blisters," said Dr. Schofield. "You'll need to stock up on Band-Aids and such."

I limped around in my new trainers. My balance was terrible and the left shoe kept slipping off because it was too big. Cleo looked to be about two sizes smaller than my other foot. But it felt so light after the weight of the cast.

Agnes handed me an insole. "Here, she said. "Put this into your trainer. It will help it from coming off."

I slipped the insole into my trainer. It worked pretty nicely.

"Let's talk about your physio exercises," Dr. Schofield said. "By now you know your exercises well. The more you do, the stronger your muscles will become and the better balance you'll have. You'll need your crutches for the first week at least, I'd say. Remember the three things we talked about: flexibility, strength, and balance."

He looked at Mom. "Time to get the stationary bike out of the basement again," he said, smiling. "That will really help again at this stage."

I looked from Cleo to Mom, to the doctor, and back again to Cleo.

"Oh, yes. The race," he said, like a mind reader. "When is it?"

"In two weeks," I said, talking to my trainers. "Two kilometers."

"I see. Okay," he said, putting his hand on my back. "Alba, if you work hard on your exercises you might be able to walk *some* of the race. But you also might have to sit this one out. Let's see how it goes, all right?"

I looked at Mom and opened my mouth to speak, but she held my gaze. "That sounds like a good idea," she said. I bit my lip and stayed quiet.

I looked down at my mismatched feet. Then I looked up at Mom and Dr. Schofield, who were beaming at each other. Mom threw her arms around him. For a horrifying second I thought they might actually *kiss*. I coughed. Loudly.

Mom's bestie Alisha came over for dinner that night. She brought Champagne, and I had ginger ale in a fancy glass. We toasted my foot and we toasted Dr. Schofield and we toasted high-performance trainers. When Alisha and Mom were fixing dinner I took the cordless telephone and went into my room. I dialed Levi's number. It rang and rang, but no one answered.

I sat on my bed and ran my finger along the scars. I moved Cleo around, left then right. I marveled at the sight of my foot pointing straight. I thought more about what Dr. Schofield said about the race.

None of it would feel real until I could show Levi.

I picked up the telephone and dialed Levi's number again. It rang and rang. This time the answering machine kicked in and Levi's mom's voice came on, saying to leave a message. I banged the receiver against my head a few times and then I hung up.

I flopped back on my bed and looked at the ceiling.

Feeling both happy and sad at the same time makes your head hurt.

Chapter Fifteen

Storm Clouds

On Saturday we took Frieda the Chihuahua to Golden Elm to visit Sadie. I like going to Golden Elm. I like the way everyone there treats my mom. The nurses and the residents give her big smiles and open their arms for her to hug them. We didn't have to sneak Frieda in because she is allowed to visit on Saturdays, when a certain supervisor isn't around.

Sadie was propped up in bed. She had breathing tubes in her nostrils. They were attached to an oxygen tank. I hesitated at the door, looking at the breathing tubes. Mom gave me a little push. "Go ahead. I'll be back in a few minutes. I want to check in on another patient."

I carried Frieda into the room and put her on the bed next to Sadie. Frieda's tail wagged like crazy and she made happy snuffle noises and burrowed into Sadie's armpit.

I watched Sadie pat Frieda, her hands knotted and her skin like tissue paper. "Silly little goose," she said to Frieda. "Is she being a good girl?" she asked.

"Yes," I said. "But she's a real hog with the petting. It's never enough."

Sadie chuckled. "A little body with big needs," she said, covering Frieda with her frail hands. "I miss her." Sadie looked at me with her soft eyes. "Thank you for my drawing—a hummingbird *charm*, how delightful."

"Yeah, it's pretty cool," I said. "Sometimes a group of hummingbirds is also called a *glittering* or a *hover*."

Sadie shook her head in wonder like it was the most amazing thing she had ever heard. "How is your foot?" she said. "Your mom told me you were getting your cast off yesterday."

I looked down at Cleo. I was wearing long stretchy leggings to cover the lily whiteness. "It doesn't look exactly... normal," I told her.

"Normal? Who wants to be *normal*?" said Sadie. "Normal is so *ordinary*." Sadie smiled. "You can't be *extraordinary*, if you're ordinary," she said with a trickle of laughter. She sighed and patted the bed for me to sit down. "We all have something that makes us feel different," she said. "Maybe it's something on the outside or something on the inside. I remember when I was a young girl like you, I thought I would fit in if I wasn't so tall." She shrugged and we smiled at each other at how silly it sounded. We petted Frieda some more.

After a while, she took my hand in hers and closed her eyes. I sat there until I realized Sadie had fallen asleep. I slipped my hand from hers gently, so as not to wake her up, and scooped Frieda from her armpit. I kissed Sadie's cheek before I left. It seemed wrong not to.

After Golden Elm, we took the dogs for a walk in the park. I left the crutches in the car and walked with Smelly and Alfred, a leash in each hand. I walked on both feet, slowly. I didn't fall but I had to keep hopping on my right foot to keep my balance. Mom sat with Frieda on a park bench and watched me with a huge smile on her face.

I walked along the path, heading for the park fountain, when I noticed a familiar figure jogging toward me through the park. It was Miranda.

"Oh, hey!" she said, reaching me. She bent over to catch her breath.

"Oh, hi," I said, wondering if these were the first words I had actually ever spoken to her.

"Wow!" she said. "Are these your dogs? How cute." Miranda knelt down and petted Smelly and Alfred. They licked her face. "You're so lucky to have dogs," she said. "I'm not allowed."

"Really? How come?" I asked.

"We live in an apartment. It doesn't allow dogs," she said. "Besides, my mom says we can't afford a pet."

I nodded, tongue-tied.

"I've seen you watching us at the track," she said, and then she laughed. Smelly kept licking her face and she laughed even harder.

I was suddenly horrified. Was she laughing at me? I pictured Miranda and her friends laughing and pointing at me in the stands. They were probably all laughing at me this whole time. At how lame I must have looked watching the athletic kids.

I pulled the dogs away and Miranda looked up, surprised. She studied my face.

"No, wait, I didn't mean...I wasn't laughing at...I just meant I saw you and—"

"It's okay," I said. "I have to go. My mom's waiting."

Miranda looked stricken. She shook her head as if she wanted to say something, but I turned and limped away. Then I couldn't help it; I looked back to see if she was still there. She was gone. She was running away from me on her perfect legs and her perfect feet.

I went back to the bench where Mom was sitting with Frieda.

"Who was that?" Mom asked.

I didn't answer. "How badly am I limping?" I asked her.

Mom shook her head, "It doesn't matter." Which is what she always says.

A bubble of anger rose up inside me.

"Why do you keep saying that?" I snapped, dropping the leashes at her feet.

"Because it doesn't matter," she said.

"But it does matter," I said. "To *me*."

"Alba, what do you want exactly? To have two good legs? To have two good feet? To walk unassisted? Well, my girl, you have all of those things. You need to remember just how lucky you are. You have to be patient. Who cares about a *limp*? Who cares about a *race*? There will be plenty of time for running once you have given your foot time to heal properly. "

"I do!" I said, suddenly raising my voice. "I care! I'm sick of having to feel lucky and patient. I just want to feel NORMAL. I don't want to limp. I want to stop being different. And I want to be in the stupid race! How can I be normal if I can't even run in a DUMB race?" The wave of anger washed through me and left me trembling.

Mom shook her head. "We talked about this, remember?" she said quietly. "About being realistic. About maybe not being able to run in the race."

I didn't answer. My heart was pounding in my ears. I picked up the dog leashes again and limped away from her. I kept hobbling, trying to ignore the stiffness, my missing balance, and the blisters that were already starting to sting. I reached the car and waited in steamy silence as Mom unlocked the backdoor to load in the dogs. I sat with them in the back seat.

We didn't go straight home. Mom pulled into the grocery store on the way.

"What should we get for dinner?" she asked, looking at me in the rearview mirror. I turned away and didn't answer because I was not talking. Especially after I wasn't allowed to sit in the car and wait with the dogs while she did the shopping. I reluctantly trailed her inside, hopping, because I refused to use my crutches.

"Let's have spaghetti with Alfredo sauce." Mom threw the ingredients into the cart. She was trying to win me over with good cooking. She was also ignoring the fact that I was ignoring her, which was beyond irritating. I followed behind her like a storm cloud. I willed myself not to feel miserable when I saw Levi's favorite spicy hummus dip with baby carrots in the cold-food aisle. I couldn't stop myself and grabbed a packet, even though no one in our house likes hummus. We arrived at the pharmacy section and I tossed box after box of different-sized Band-Aids in the cart.

"Hey there, big spender," Mom said, replacing the boxes on the shelves. "How about we start with one box?"

I kept throwing Band-Aid boxes into the cart.

"Alba, stop!" Mom said. "I didn't raise you to behave this way. To sulk and feel sorry for yourself." She sighed and lowered her voice. "Put the boxes back now, please."

For the second time that day I turned my back on my mom and went to the car.

On the way home I hoped that Mom would insist on stopping by Levi's, but then I realized that she wouldn't because we had the dogs in the car and groceries in the trunk.

I looked out of the window.

All I could see was Miranda and her friends laughing at me.

Chapter Sixteen

The Story of the Hummingbird and the Fire

At dinner I continued my snooty mood and only spoke when absolutely necessary. I could tell this was grinding on Mom's last nerve. I was finally allowed to go to my room after I cleared the plates.

In my room I flopped on the bed and looked up at the glow-in-the-dark star stickers that Levi and I had put up years ago. I wondered what a wormhole sticker would look like. Then I noticed something on my pillow. It was a folded-up piece of paper with a ribbon tied around it. I sat up, untied the ribbon, and unwrapped the paper. It was a story typed on a single sheet of plain, white paper. The title read: *The Story of the Hummingbird and the Fire.*

I went back into the kitchen where Mom was doing the dishes. I waved the paper at her. "Did Levi drop this over?" I asked her. "Or is it from Sadie?"

Mom shrugged. It was her turn for the silent treatment. All she would say was, "It's a surprise." She gave me the look adults give you when they want you to figure things out for yourself.

I took the paper back to my room and put it on my desk. I tried my best to ignore it, but it kept calling to me. It's hard to keep up a bad mood when you're alone. So I grabbed the paper, sat on my bed, and started to read.

Long, long ago in an ancient land, a huge fire swept the entire forest. The fire ate up all of the trees and all of the grass and all of the shrubs. Black smoke darkened the sky. All of the animals in the forest ran for their lives away from the fire. It was a mad stampede toward safety, away from the flames.

But the hummingbird flew in the opposite direction. She flew toward the fire, her beak full of water. Once she had dropped the bead of water onto the forest fire, she flew back to the river to fill her tiny beak and return to the fire. She repeated this over and over.

"What are you doing, silly hummingbird?" the large animals called up to her. "You are too little; your wings will burn;

your beak is too small to hold enough water."

But the hummingbird did not listen. She kept returning again and again to the river, each time flying back to deliver a single drop of water on the fire.

"Do you really believe you can put out this huge fire?" the large animals called up to her. "With your little wings and your small beak? What you're doing will barely make a difference."

The hummingbird stopped and perched on a branch. She was tired and her feathers were blackened with soot. She looked down at the big animals and spoke with her tiny voice.

"I am doing what I can," she said.

I folded up the paper the way I had found it, tied the ribbon around it, and slipped it under my pillow. Levi must have dropped off the story while we were at the park or shopping.

Hummingbirds were our code. Hummingbirds were what had made us friends in the first place.

I got the telephone handset from the living room and brought it back to my room. I dialed the number and waited. The line picked up and I heard the familiar, wheezy breath at the other end.

I open my mouth to talk, but the words got stuck. I gripped the receiver, listening to the wheezy breath at the other end, the wheezy breath that was waiting for me to speak. I waited too long to say anything. I felt stupid and hung up. The worst thing was that he must have known it was me.

He knew it was me and he didn't say anything either.

Chapter Seventeen

A Golden Elm Celebrity

I was still not talking to Mom when she gave me a pair of skinny jeans on Monday morning. She handed them to me at breakfast.

"I wish I were giving these to you when you had a better attitude," she said. "But it was my plan to give them to you this morning, so here you go."

I unfolded the jeans, held them up, and looked them over. Then I refolded them into my lap. "I don't want to go to school today," I told her. "I don't want to go back until I can go without the crutches."

Mom sat back in her seat and looked at me. Her eyes softened. She took a deep breath, leaned forward, and reached for my hand.

"I understand," she said. "But your physio is going to take some time. Your first session is after school today."

"But can't I start the physio now instead of going to school?" I asked. "Please? Can't I just work on my physio until I can walk properly? Then I will go back to school. Please?"

Mom sighed. "Wait here," she said. "I have an idea."

Mom took the phone into her room and closed the door. I played with my toast, cutting it into smaller and smaller triangles. After ten minutes she came back out again.

"Okay, I think we have a solution," she said. "Dr. Schofield knows the physiotherapist at Golden Elm. He says he will speak with her about the physio you need to do. If she is willing, and I can clear it with Golden Elm and your school, you can do your rehab with me at work."

"Yes!" I said, throwing my arms to the ceiling. "Thank you!"

"Okay, hang on a minute. I have to find out if Golden Elm and the school will allow it. Just eat your breakfast." She looked at my geometric toast and made a face at me.

She got on the phone again while I crossed my fingers and waited. After what seemed like a century, but was in actual fact twenty-three minutes, Mom hung up the phone.

"We are in business," she said. "Evelyn, the physiotherapist at Golden Elm, has spoken with Dr. Schofield. She is happy to supervise your physio, but her responsibilities are to the residents first, okay? You will have to listen and do what she says without any back talk. Understand?"

I hugged her. "I promise I won't get in anyone's way," I said. "I promise I will listen and do everything Evelyn says. I promise."

"Principal Ibrahim will give us a homework package that you can work on for the week. We can pick it up at the end of the day. No falling behind, okay?"

"I promise," I said again, still clinging to her.

Mom stroked my cheek. "I'm not sure why I didn't think of this earlier. Besides, Sadie and the others will love it."

I was pretty famous by the end of my rehab at Golden Elm. All of the folks there understood how much I wanted to walk without crutches. This was a goal they could totally get behind. I had the best pep squad ever. Every day my ankle felt less stiff and my foot and leg got stronger.

The Golden Elm physiotherapist, Evelyn, was super nice. She showed me some new exercises to help strengthen the muscles in my foot, ankle, and calf. I also used the stationary bike to help stretch the muscles. I even joined in the seniors' yoga class.

"Yoga is excellent for balance and strength," Evelyn told me.

I spent hours on the exercise bike and on my strengthening exercises. By the third day I could actually do the Tree Pose, balancing on Cleo for three seconds in a row.

In between my workouts I went to visit Sadie.

"Do a runway walk," she'd say, and I would prance around her room, showing her Cleo's improvement each day.

One day I told Sadie about the bee hummingbird. The bee hummingbird is the smallest bird in the world. It is native to Cuba and measures only two inches long. They make nests from cobwebs and lay eggs the size of peas.

Sadie could not hear enough about the bee hummingbird. I borrowed Mom's laptop and found YouTube clips of the bee hummingbird to show Sadie. We watched them hover and dip on their gossamer wings, their tiny heads flashing green and pink in the sunlight.

Sadie watched the clips with a huge smile. "I always knew fairies were real," she said.

Sometimes Sadie fell asleep during my visits, so I would go back to my physio exercises or do my homework or wander around making new friends.

I had afternoon tea with the residents in the recreational room and learned how to properly dunk the cookies into the milky tea without losing half of it. I watched too many daytime dramas. I made a poster of hummingbird facts and pinned it up on the community board. The residents were so jazzed about the poster that I promised to give a presentation at a later date.

I kept my hummingbird story in my pocket all the while. It became worn at the corners from so much folding and unfolding.

The day I could finally walk the entire length of the Golden Elm corridor without my crutches, without grabbing for balance, or without hopping, the residents stood in their doorways and cheered. Sadie clapped from her bed.

When Mom and I went to see Dr. Schofield, he said he was super impressed with my progress. "You're made of tough stuff, cowgirl," he said. "But you'll still have to come and see me a day or two before your race. We'll see how you're doing and how you can participate, okay?"

The whole time away from school, every night before I went to sleep, I curled up with the dogs and thought about being normal. I thought about being in the race. I thought about brave little hummingbirds. I thought about space-time traveling librarians.

Mostly I tried to stop missing Levi.

Chapter Eighteen

Day of the Skinny Jeans

On the day I was ready to go back to school, I slipped on the skinny jeans that Mom had given me. I stared at myself in the mirror. With the jeans on, no one would even be able to tell what was underneath. If I wanted to, I could hide Cleo forever. I walked back and forth, trying to see how much I still limped. I left my crutches at home.

I arrived at the school gate with butterflies in my stomach. Kids were used to seeing me the other way. Now I looked normal, but I didn't *feel* normal. This wasn't how I had expected it would be at all. I felt like I stuck out even more. I stood outside the gate, chewing on my lip, watching the kids in the schoolyard. Groups of kids—two, three, or four—had their heads together, laughing and talking, telling each other stories about their weekends. *How do you break into a friend-pod?* I didn't have a clue how it could be done. It had been much easier to make friends at Golden Elm.

Eventually I walked inside the gate. I kept my eyes on the ground. When I looked up, I noticed kids look at me and then look away. Did I look ridiculous? Did I look normal? How bad was my limp? I reached for my crutches before remembering that I didn't have them anymore. It was hard to believe this was the moment I had been working so hard toward. The moment I had been dreaming about my whole life.

I looked around but I didn't see Levi anywhere. Then I remembered it was the day for his chess team to play at the annual chess championship.

In the classroom I sat at my desk, but I couldn't concentrate on anything Ms. Wright was saying. All I could think about was Cleo under my desk.

"Find a partner for group work," I heard Ms. Wright say.

I looked around the classroom. Everyone else had paired up except me. The teacher came to my desk.

"Alba, would you like some help finding a partner?" she said.

The only thing worse than group work was the teacher having to find a partner for you.

"Alba, sit here with Stephanie and Olivia," said Ms. Wright. "This activity will be fine with three."

Stephanie Dorset and Olivia Demarco were sitting together at the desk in front of me. The girls exchanged a look but were perfectly nice and moved over to make room for me. I wanted them to say something about Cleo, about how great it was that I didn't have a cast anymore, that I wasn't using crutches. But at the same time I didn't want anyone to look at me. I slunk down low in my seat.

"Trivia questions!" said Ms. Wright. "I am going to call out a question and you can consult with your partner. Or partners," she said, looking at me. "Put up your hand once you have an answer."

On a normal day Levi and I would have loved this game.

"First question," said Ms. Wright. "Can you name three countries in Central America?"

I thought of my hummingbird migration poster at home and I knew that I could easily name three countries. But I couldn't speak.

"You know this, right?" Stephanie said to me. "I remember from your eco-project."

"Yeah, don't you know, like, all the bird places in Central America?" Olivia added.

I got tongue-tied and flushed red. Before I had time to spit out the country names, another group beat us to it.

"I'm sorry," I said to Stephanie and Olivia. "I guess I'm not feeling well. You guys go ahead without me."

I left the class and hid in the washroom until the lunch recess bell.

At lunch recess, I ate my lunch alone and then went to the school office.

"Can I do the recycle bins?" I asked the office staff.

"No need, Alba," said the office administrator. "You should go outside to play."

Ms. Sharma said the same thing when I went to see if she had been sucked into another dimension. She was alive and well, and stamping library books.

"Alba," she said, looking up from the books. "Look at you! You look great!" She sat beaming at me. "It must be wonderful to have your cast off."

I nodded and tried to smile back. "Thanks," I said. "I was just wondering if you needed help today."

"Not today," she said, returning to her work. "Besides, you must be dying to get out there in the playground now, right?"

"Right!" I said, making an effort to sound enthusiastic for her sake. "Just thought I'd check."

She waved as I left. "Have fun!"

Coach Adams's office door was closed and locked.

I went outside eventually and sat down on the bench that Levi and I use. After a while Miranda came over. She stood in front of me, resting a basketball on her hip.

"Do you want to play four square?" She asked.

Her niceness flustered me. "I'm busy," I blurted. *Busy?* How lame was that.

Was Miranda asking me to play so that she and her friends could laugh at me? I wasn't going to risk it. I kept my beet-red face on her orange trainers until they walked away.

I glared at my skinny jeans. I blamed Mom for giving them to me and for making me look so dumb. Not one kid had said anything about Cleo.

At the end of the day, I walked home slowly. I felt more and more miserable with each step.

At home I went straight to my room and took off the skinny jeans. I screwed them up into a ball and threw them into the back of my closet. Then I buried my face in dog fur and cried. The dogs assembled in my room, watching me, taking turns being my cry mat.

After a while I wiped my tears on a scarf. I held the scarf in my hand and remembered Abigail and her trick. *What the heck?* I thought. I babbled my troubles into the scarf, then I put it in the washing machine.

Abigail's mother was right. Strangely it helped to make me feel a little better.

I unfolded my hummingbird story and reread it a few more times. Then I got on the exercise bike. After that I did my physio exercises and practiced the Tree Pose.

Before I went to sleep, I got my skinny jeans from the back of the closet and smoothed them out on the bed, ready for the next day.

Chapter Nineteen

Love at First Sight

The next morning I saw my first hummingbird.

It was a male and he was perched on a branch in our cherry tree in the backyard. I could tell it was male by the flash of bright purple feathers around his neck. Only the males have the bright feathers. He was alone. Hummingbirds generally migrate solo. He sat beautifully still, his tiny body and feathers glittering in the early sunshine.

"Hey there, stranger," I said quietly. "What took you so long? I've been waiting for you all spring."

The hummingbird alighted from the branch and hovered at one of the sugar-water feeders. After a few seconds he returned to his branch. He appeared to cock his head and stare directly at me. He seemed to be saying, *Me? I could be asking* you *the same question.*

I wrote in my field-notes booklet and then I went inside and put the booklet in my backpack. I threw the backpack over my shoulder and grabbed my lunch. I told Mom I was leaving for school.

"So early?" she said.

"There's something I am late for," I said.

I went on the school bus and got off at the stop close to Levi's house. I walked to his house and looked at his door. I knocked and waited, I knocked again.

Levi opened the door like he had been waiting there for me all of this time. We stared at each other for a while.

"How was the chess tournament?" I asked him.

"We won," Levi said with a shrug.

"I saw my first hummingbird this morning," I said, handing him my field-notes booklet. "He was alone. He was perched in the cherry tree."

Levi took the booklet and looked it over. He nodded. "They like to perch," said Levi. "They spend most of their lives perching, in fact."

"Hummingbirds don't like to walk," I said. "Their feet are too small to walk."

Levi looked up from the page and gave me a small smile. "Flying is their most favorite thing, I guess." He handed me back the field-studies booklet. "They excel at flight."

"I've missed them," I said. "I thought maybe none would come this year."

"It is highly unlikely that would occur," said Levi, looking me in the eye. "I cannot imagine that ever happening."

We stood staring at each other.

So much had happened, but Levi still looked the same. He still looked like his usual, crazy-smart, kind, freckly self. He still looked like my best friend.

"Do you want to go to school together today?" I asked him.

"Sure," said Levi. Then he pointed to Cleo and said, "I like your jeans." As if it was nothing at all.

And just like that, it happened.

Happiness, like hummingbirds, can land in your heart.

Chapter Twenty

The Break In

Our class had silent reading time in the library that morning. As we filed past Ms. Sharma's office, we noticed she wasn't there. Levi and I exchanged looks. Once we were settled into our beanbags, I passed Levi a note: *Supply Closet.*

He sent back: *Affirmative.*

So what do we do?

Break into the supply closet.

You're cray cray. How?

Tools.

When?

Today.

?!?!?!?!

Critical!! I've been waiting for you. We can't wait any longer.

Okay. What tools?

Meet me at the library. Give me ten minutes.

Okay.

P.S. Eat this paper!

When the lunch bell rang we nodded at each other. I packed up our books and watched Levi trot out of the library. I decided to go and eat my lunch while I waited. Mom had made my favorite kind of bagel and I was hungry—cosmic emergency or not. By the time I got back to the library, Levi was already there, standing outside the double doors. His face looked frozen—with either fear or excitement, I couldn't tell which.

"Jeez!" I said, pointing to the screwdriver. "Where did you get *that*?"

"Janitor's closet," he said, giving it a timid wave.

"We are going to get in such deep trouble," I mumbled.

"We *have* to do it," said Levi. "Or we'll never know. Not for sure."

"Please breathe, Levi," I said.

Levi peered into the library. "Her lights are off," he said. "Come on."

We crept through the library and stood outside Ms. Sharma's office door.

"Here goes," I said, gripping the door handle. I opened it slowly as Levi wheezed behind me. We went into the dark office and moved closer and closer to the supply closet.

"Wait," I whispered. "We should leave a note or something. What if we get sucked in?"

We looked around Ms. Sharma's desk for some paper and a pen. Levi wrote a note, his writing all jiggly because his hand was trembling so much.

If you are reading this it means we are in danger due to a space-time warp in the supply closet. Please send help!
Yours truly,
Levi and Alba

"Okay, good," I said. "Let's go." I walked to the supply closet and put my hand on the handle. The closet handle was warm. I pulled it gently. Locked. I tugged a little harder. Still locked.

"Okay," I said to Levi. "Your turn."

Levi stepped up with the screwdriver and began to fiddle the lock with it. I thought I could actually hear our hearts beating.

Suddenly we heard a thump from inside the closet. We jumped back. More thumping was coming from behind the closet door. Then the closet door was opening! A slice of light appeared.

The door opened wider and Levi screamed.

"Shhh, shhh, children, children, it's okay." It was Ms. Sharma. "Nothing to be frightened of. It's just me."

It took us a little while to focus. Ms. Sharma sat down inside the big closet, legs crossed, on a large comfortable cushion. She was smiling at us. There was a little night-light plugged into the socket in the closet and we could see the walls were pasted with scenery posters—mountains, ocean, and trees. It was beautiful in there. It smelled of incense, the same sandalwood incense that Alisha burns in her apartment. It was the smell I had detected the first time I snooped in Ms. Sharma's office.

"This is my meditation closet," she said. "Here," she added, reaching for my hand. "Help me up."

Ms. Sharma climbed out of her closet and switched on the lights to her office. She was barefoot. "I'm sorry if I frightened you," said Ms. Sharma. "Were you worried?"

"We, we, we..." Levi was having trouble getting his words out.

I felt Levi's back to make sure he was still breathing.

"We saw you go into your office and disappear," I said. "We...we thought there must be some kind of—" Then it was my turn to be stuck. I cleared my throat. "We thought there was a wormhole to another dimension in the supply closet."

Levi handed her the note.

Ms. Sharma chuckled. "I guess you could call it that," she said. "But not quite."

She put a hand on each of our shoulders. "I meditate. It is an important daily practice for me. Since I had my baby, it is hard to get peace and quiet at home. And once the baby has gone to sleep, I am too tired. So you see, I had this idea to make a meditation closet here."

"But it was locked," said Levi.

"Yes, I have a little latch inside," she said. "So I won't be disturbed."

Levi and I exchange looks. Disturbing her is exactly what we had done.

"We're sorry," I said.

"Are we in trouble?" asked Levi.

Ms. Sharma shook her head. "No, but you know that entering a teacher's office without permission is not allowed, yes?" She reached for the screwdriver and gently released it from Levi's grip. "Not to mention taking things from the janitor's closet and tampering with locks."

Levi gulped. "It was my fault," he spluttered. "It was all my idea."

"You are good children," she said. "I know you didn't mean any harm." She smiled. "But promise me you will come and ask me directly next time you think I am being transported to another world." She giggled. "Okay?"

We nodded.

"Okay, out for lunch now," she said, slipping her feet into her shoes. She ushered us toward the library exit. "Who ever said the library was boring?"

As we were leaving, Ms. Sharma put her hand on Levi's arm. "By the way, Levi," she said. "What's the difference between science fiction and nonfiction?"

"Facts," Levi mumbled to his feet.

"No. The real difference is made by curious minds like yours," she said. "People who have no boundary to their curiosity. People who are brave enough to imagine, to explore, to invent, and to find answers. Isaac Asimov, the famous author and scientist, said, 'Today's science fiction is tomorrow's science fact.' Remember, less than one hundred years ago, a book about exploring space would have been science fiction." She smiled at us. "Maybe nothing is impossible, given enough time."

We left the library and stood out in the hall. To my surprise, when I turned to look at Levi, he had a grin that stretched from ear to ear.

"You're not disappointed?" I asked him.

Levi shook his head with a goofy smile on his face, which was contagious, because I felt myself begin to smile back. Maybe it was from the excitement of our first break-and-enter crime. Or maybe it was the weirdness of finding our librarian barefoot in the supply closet. Or maybe we were in shock or something, but we both started to giggle. Pretty soon we were doubled over, our sides aching, delirious with laughter. We couldn't stop. Bent over, bumping into each other, hysterical. We laughed and laughed until we couldn't breathe.

And after a while, once I had caught my breath again, I stood up and realized what was so funny.

Chapter Twenty-one

The Hummingbird Theory

"Well, cowgirl," said Dr. Schofield. "I've got to tell you that I am very impressed with the rehab you have managed to do in such a short amount of time."

Mom and I were in the doctor's office. He was examining Cleo.

"The race is in two days," I said.

"I know," he said. Dr. Schofield looked up at me. "The good news," he said, "is that you can participate in the race." He paused. "But perhaps not in the way you hoped. Even though you have done a fine job strengthening and stretching your muscles and working on your balance, it is just too soon to run for such a long distance. It would be too strenuous. It has only been two weeks. By the end of the summer you will be able to run for a good long distance. But a two-kilometer race at this stage is just too soon."

I didn't say anything, I just nodded.

"I will send a note to your school recommending that you *walk* the race for up to one kilometer."

I nodded again and felt Mom's hand on the top of my head.

"It might not be the exact news you were hoping for, Alba, but I want you to know that the work you have done to get your foot and leg in this shape is remarkable," he said. "You should be very proud of yourself."

"We are very proud," said Mom.

I listened to the words and nodded, and tried to keep the good and bad news balanced in my head so the tears wouldn't spill out.

On race day I woke up super early. It was warm. Warm enough to wear shorts. I got dressed and looked at myself in the mirror. I looked at my mismatched legs in the orange trainers, and I pictured Miranda's perfect long, brown legs coming out of the same shoes.

Coach Adams had mapped out a walking route for me after Dr. Schofield sent a note saying that I could only walk the race. Coach Adams drew me a walking circuit around the school, and he said it should have me at the finish line at around the same time as the final runners.

"You'll need a walking buddy," he said. "School rules."

"I'm working on it," I told him.

Before I got to school I dropped by Levi's house. He opened the door and smiled. "Hey," he said. "Want some breakfast?"

"Not if it's porridge," I said, following him into the kitchen. It smelled of pancakes.

Levi sliced a banana on top of my pancake and poured maple syrup all over it. We sat together at the kitchen table eating our breakfast. A copy of *A Brief History of Time* sat next to Levi's plate.

"I'm sorry I said the wormhole was a stupid idea. It wasn't stupid. I'm sorry I called you a nerd." I pointed to his book. "Ms. Sharma is right," I said. "One day it will be you writing something like that. And that's not weird at all. It's cool. "

Levi smiled. "Thanks," he said. Then he looked at me sheepishly. "I shouldn't have been so unsupportive about you wanting to be in the race," he said. "That's the word my mom used."

"Actually, that's kind of why I came this morning," I told him. "I have a favor to ask you."

I told Levi that I was going to walk the race. I showed him the map that Coach Adams had made me.

"So I told Coach Adams that I would ask if you could be the timekeeper instead of me. I know it means you need to be outside, but it's not for very long. Can you do it?"

"I don't think so," he said.

"Levi, I should never have said that you were scared to go outside," I said. "It was mean. Don't let that be the reason, okay? Please?"

"Sorry," was all he would say.

At race time Levi could not be found. I helped Coach Adams hand out the running bibs.

All of the runners lined up at the starting line, jostling each other. The youngest kids were in the front and the older ones at the back. Everyone was so excited that Coach Adams had to blow his whistle three times for quiet. The teachers who were running moved among the crowd, trying to get the kids to simmer down. Principal Ibrahim held up a megaphone and a race gun.

"Are we ready?" she called, and the crowd cheered and then eventually grew silent.

"Get ready! Get set!" she paused. "Go!"

The kids tumbled past us in a jumble of arms and legs. When the last runner had finally straggled by I made my way to the school gate to meet up with my walking buddies. Mom was there waiting. She handed me the leashes.

"This is Alfred and this is Smelly," I said to Coach Adams.

He bent down and gave each dog a pat. "Well, I guess eight legs beat two," he said, looking up and giving us a wink.

"They'll take good care of her," said Mom. "Don't worry."

Coach Adams nodded and smiled. "I'm sure they will," he said. "Do you have your map?" he asked, turning to me. I patted my pocket where it sat folded up next to my hummingbird story.

"Okay, you're all set, Alba," he said, giving me a high-five. "See you at the finish line!"

I held a leash in each hand and started off at a good pace. I kept walking and didn't look back at Mom and Coach Adams. I knew they were still watching me.

It was a beautiful day. Even though I was walking, and not running with all the other kids, it felt good to be in the race. It wasn't how I imagined it would be, but I had worked hard for it. Cleo was stronger every day, but it still didn't take long for me to get tired and for my blisters to start hurting.

"Let's slow down," I said to the dogs, once the school was out of sight. I hopped on my good foot every now and again to take the weight off the blisters. At the bottom of the first hill, before the street curved, I saw a familiar figure. It was Levi. He was standing by the path, holding out a bottle of water like you see volunteers do at marathons.

I stopped to take the bottle. "Is this why you couldn't be timekeeper?"

"I thought you would need proper hydration," he said.

I bumped my shoulder against his and he looked at his feet.

"How far is it?" he asked, giving his inhaler a nervous pat. "Maybe I'll come along."

I pulled out the map. "Here, you can be navigator," I said, which pepped him up a lot.

We speed-walked—or tried to—with Levi barking out the directions loudly. We had finally reached the halfway point when I said to Levi, "Hey, thanks for sending me the story."

"What story?" said Levi.

"The hummingbird story," I said.

Levi shook his head. "I didn't," he said.

"Really?" I said. "That's so weird." Then I realized it made perfect sense.

"Tell it to me," he said.

And so, for the rest of the way, we walked and I told Levi the hummingbird story.

At the end of the story Levi clapped and I took a bow.

"That's awesome," he said.

"Levi," I said. "What is the Theory of Everything?"

Levi started to walk again, his head down, thinking. "The Theory of Everything is the ultimate goal of science," he said. "It's a single theory that will describe the entire universe."

"Well, I think I have my own theory," I said. "The Theory of Hummingbirds."

Levi raised his eyebrows.

"Well, hummingbirds don't sit around moaning about their tiny feet and the fact that they can't walk. Hummingbirds don't sit on their perch worrying they are too small to make a difference in the world. They don't care that the entire animal kingdom is bigger than them. Like the hummingbird in the story, she just does what she can."

Levi was nodding. "So what's the theory?" he asked.

"The Theory of Hummingbirds," I said, "is to just be who you are and do the best you can." I stopped walking and tapped my head to think some more. "No, wait. LOVE who you are and LOVE what you can do."

Levi gave me a nod of approval. "I like it," he said. "A lot."

I'd been so absorbed with our conversation that it had taken my mind off how much Cleo was hurting. Now we could see the school and some runners arriving from the other direction and streaming through the gates.

"Look," said Levi, pointing ahead.

Someone was jumping up and down and waving to us from the school entrance.

"It's Miranda," I said. Miranda was clapping and jumping and gesturing to us.

"Should we go for it?" I asked.

"Nothing," said Levi, raising a fist in the air, "is impossible!"

We picked up our walking pace until we reached Miranda. She high-fived us. "You guys are doing great!" She said. "Come on! Just a little way to the finish! Let's go!" She jogged alongside us. I sped up a little until I was jogging with Levi and Miranda toward the finish line. The dogs got excited and pulled me along.

Then I wasn't jogging, I was *running*.

I was running and laughing, and bumping shoulders with the other runners, just like I had pictured in my mind on practice day when I had watched Miranda win.

As the finish line got closer and closer I could hear more people cheering and clapping. My heart was pounding and Cleo was screaming and my blisters were burning, but I was really doing it. I was not watching the race, I was *in* the race.

I dropped the leashes and raised my arms as we crossed the finish line. Then I collapsed, out of breath, on the grass, still laughing. Levi flung himself on the ground next to me. He took a pump of his inhaler. "I'm never doing that again," he gasped, making me laugh even harder. We rolled around on the cool grass, laughing and gulping for air. The dogs bounced around us, licking our faces and yipping.

"We did it!" I shouted up at the sky.

Miranda sat on the grass with us, petting the dogs. She giggled when the dogs licked her face. She was wearing the winner ribbon.

"Hey, great race," she told me. "Nice finish." She smiled and pointed at our matching trainers. "Nice shoes!"

"Thanks," I said, sitting up. I gripped Miranda's hand and pumped her arm up and down. "Congratulations," I said, pointing to her ribbon.

"Oh, thanks," she said with a shrug. "But, it's nothing compared to you." She paused. "I heard you tell the coach that day that you wanted to race. I thought you were so brave." She shook her head. "I'm sorry. It's dumb. I just never knew how to talk to you. I was embarrassed or scared that I would upset you or something. I was never laughing at you, I promise."

"I know. You're not dumb," I said. "It's my fault. I've been kind of a jerk lately."

We sat shaking hands and looking at each other. Then Miranda took her winner ribbon from her own t-shirt and stuck it onto mine. She was either the nicest person on the planet and wanted to be my friend or she wanted me to quit pumping her arm so hard.

"Do you want to help me walk the dogs after school sometimes?" I asked her.

Miranda face lit up. "That would be awesome," she said. "Thanks."

"I've got to go now," she said, standing up and pointing to her friends. "But I'll see you tomorrow, right?"

"Great!" I said. "See you tomorrow." I stood up and waved good-bye. When I helped Levi to his feet, he was breathing fine again.

"Are you okay?" I asked him.

He nodded. "Never better," he said, stretching his arms out wide and looking up to the sky. "As a matter of fact I feel surprisingly good."

Once we were on our feet, we saw my mom and Levi's mom clapping in the stands. Then I noticed that Dr. Schofield was there too. He was cheering and clapping like his life depended on it. They all came down from the stands to join us.

"That was impressive!" Dr. Schofield said. He bent down next to me and looked at Cleo. "Do you mind?" he asked. I nodded and he took off my trainer to give Cleo a look over, being careful not to touch the blisters. "You're one tough customer," he said with a wink. "Well done, cowgirl."

Mom pulled out her cell phone to take a picture. "Stand together," she said. Levi and I bent in next to the dogs for the photo. "Say hummingbirds!" she said.

After the photo I threw my arms around her waist and I breathed in her apple shampoo. "Thank you for the story," I whispered in her ear.

Chapter Twenty-two

The Best Place in the Universe

Levi and I asked our moms if we could go out for burgers together to celebrate.

"Great idea," said Mom. "Let's get going. I'm starving."

Dr. Schofield said he had better go because he was on his way to pick up Geffrey and Michael. "But I wouldn't have missed this for the world," he said.

I looked at Dr. Schofield and my mom smiling at each other.

"Do you want to come with us for burgers too?" I asked him. "Maybe you can bring Geffrey and Michael. I'd really like to meet them."

Dr. Schofield and my mom exchanged a happy look.

"I'd love to," he said, squeezing my arm. "In fact, that sounds like the best invitation I've had for a long time." He looked at Mom. "I'll just go and get the boys and meet you there."

I leaned on Mom as we walked out of the schoolyard to the car.

"I like Dr. Schofield," I said to her.

"Me too," said Mom, kissing the top of my head. "Me too."

We dropped in at home so I could change out of my running shorts. I took off my trainers and had a good look at Cleo in the mirror. With more hard work, my limp will disappear. But my legs will never match. Cleo will always be sizes smaller.

I studied my scars, my skinny leg, and my small foot, and I knew that it didn't matter what I looked like. Cleo didn't have to be normal, because it wasn't normal that mattered.

Levi and I had been laughing so hard after we found Ms. Sharma in the closet because we finally got it. Neither of us had found what we were looking for. Levi didn't find his wormhole and I didn't find normal. But it didn't matter. We were together.

The best place in the universe was under our feet the whole time.

The End

Glossary of Alba's Hummingbird Facts

Hummingbirds can't walk.

Their feet are too tiny. They perch, but never walk. Hummingbirds are built for flight. Small feet are light and reduce aerodynamic drag. They can hop sideways on a branch, and perch for long periods, but do not walk.

Hummingbirds hear better than humans.

Hummingbirds have highly acute hearing. They need good hearing to communicate and to attract a mate. Some male hummingbirds even have ear tufts to impress the females.

Hummingbirds have zero sense of smell.

Hummingbirds have little or no sense of smell. The plants and flowers they rely on for nectar have no fragrance. They use their eyesight to find the nectar.

Hummingbirds weigh the same as a penny.

The smallest bird, the bee hummingbird, weighs as little as .06 ounces. A penny weighs .09 ounces.

Hummingbirds can fly over 3,000 miles every year for migration.

The longest migration on record is a female rufous hummingbird that flew from Florida to Alaska. That is 3,250 miles!

A group of hummingbirds is called a charm, a glittering, or a hover.

Another name for a group of hummingbirds is a *troubling*.

Hummingbirds have the highest metabolism of all animals.

The hummingbird's efficient energy system is needed to sustain their rapid heart rate and wing speed. To conserve energy they can enter a hibernation-like state called *torpor* when they are not feeding.

Hummingbirds are not social and have been known to attack other birds.

Hummingbirds are little birds with big attitudes! Hummingbirds will show aggression if they feel their nests or feeding areas are being threatened. An angry hummingbird will chirp; dive; chase its opponent; and in rare cases, use its beak as a weapon.

The color red attracts hummingbirds.

Hummingbirds have terrific sight. They see every color humans do, but they also see ultraviolet light, so colors appear to be even more vivid. There is no scientific proof that hummingbirds are attracted to the color red, but they seem to favor the nectar of flowers that are red. Also, because bird feeders are usually red, it could be that hummingbirds have developed a conditioned response to the color.

Hummingbird migration.

If you live in North America, you may see a hummingbird as early as February (southern states). In the northern states of America, and in Canada, sightings are more usual in mid- to late May.

The bee hummingbird is the smallest bird in the world. They make nests from cobwebs and lay eggs the size of peas.

The Bee Hummingbird is the smallest living bird in the world. It is native to Cuba and measures only 2 to 2½ inches long. The largest hummingbird is called the giant hummingbird and grows up to 8½ inches in length. It lives in the Andes Mountain Range of South America.

Only the males have bright feathers.

Male hummingbirds have bright feathers to attract a mate and to signal dominance to other males. The patch of bright feathers on the males' neck is called a *gorget*. Females are usually brown or green.

Hummingbirds migrate alone.

Hummingbirds make the long migration journey alone, often on the same flight path they have used before. They fly quite low, just above treetops or water. Young hummingbirds must find their own way without the guidance of their parents.

They excel in flight.

Hummingbirds are the acrobats of the bird world. Not only do they fly forward, but also backward, sideways, and straight up. And they can dive and hover. They can even fly upside down!

Author's Note

Like Alba, I was born with a clubfoot. Congenital *talipes equinovarus* (CTEV), commonly known as clubfoot, affects many children. One in every 1,000 babies in the United States is born with the condition. Treatment usually begins at birth with a series of bracing and casting. Most are responsive to this method and do not require surgery. In more difficult cases surgery is required. In my instance, the treatments and surgeries were completed before I started the first grade. I was fortunate that I did not experience reoccurrence as I grew older, but it can often be the situation. Alba is a fictional character, but she represents the children who require further treatment as they grow.

It was my experience of having CTEV that prompted me to write *The Theory of Hummingbirds*. But I suspect we all have something that makes us feel different; something that we might struggle with to gain self-acceptance. In writing the story I hope to honor the differences within us, whatever the diversity may be.

In the story, a parable about a hummingbird helps Alba to embrace her challenges. The hummingbird has symbolic significance to many indigenous cultures in South, Central, and North America. *The Hummingbird and the Fire* is a parable that is told all over the world. The origins of the tale are believed to be from the ancient Quechua culture in Peru, where the story is used to impart the importance of caring for the environment, no matter how insignificant the action may appear to be.

Or as Alba would say, *Love who you are and love what you can do.*

Acknowledgments

Giant wingspans of thanks to many who have helped Alba's story take flight.

To my friend Chandra Wohleber, I send my deepest gratitude. Without Chandra's gentle guidance on early drafts the project would never have left the ground.

Huge thanks to Ann Featherstone, Gail Winskill, Erin Alladin, and the brilliant team at Pajama Press—it is a dream come true to find a home with Pajama. Thanks to my writing group, Joyce Grant, Nancy Miller, and Gary Kohl, for their unwavering encouragement.

Thanks to the Ontario Arts Council for their financial support.

Thanks to Adam Tarvit, Health and Physical Education Teacher at Toronto's Withrow Avenue Junior Public School, for his intel on elementary school cross-country races.

Special thanks to Dr. Andrew Howard, Paediatric Orthopaedic Surgeon, Toronto, for his invaluable insights and information on current paediatric treatments, surgery, and rehabilitation. Any errors are my own.

I am indebted to the awe-inspiring work of Stephen Hawking and his brilliant *A Brief History of Time*.

This book is dedicated to my mother, Judith Margaret. I wish to also remember my late father Ebet and send a shout-out to my amazing siblings Valerie, Rani, Andre, and Julia.

And finally, boundless love to my beautiful family, Sophia, Teddy, and Mark.